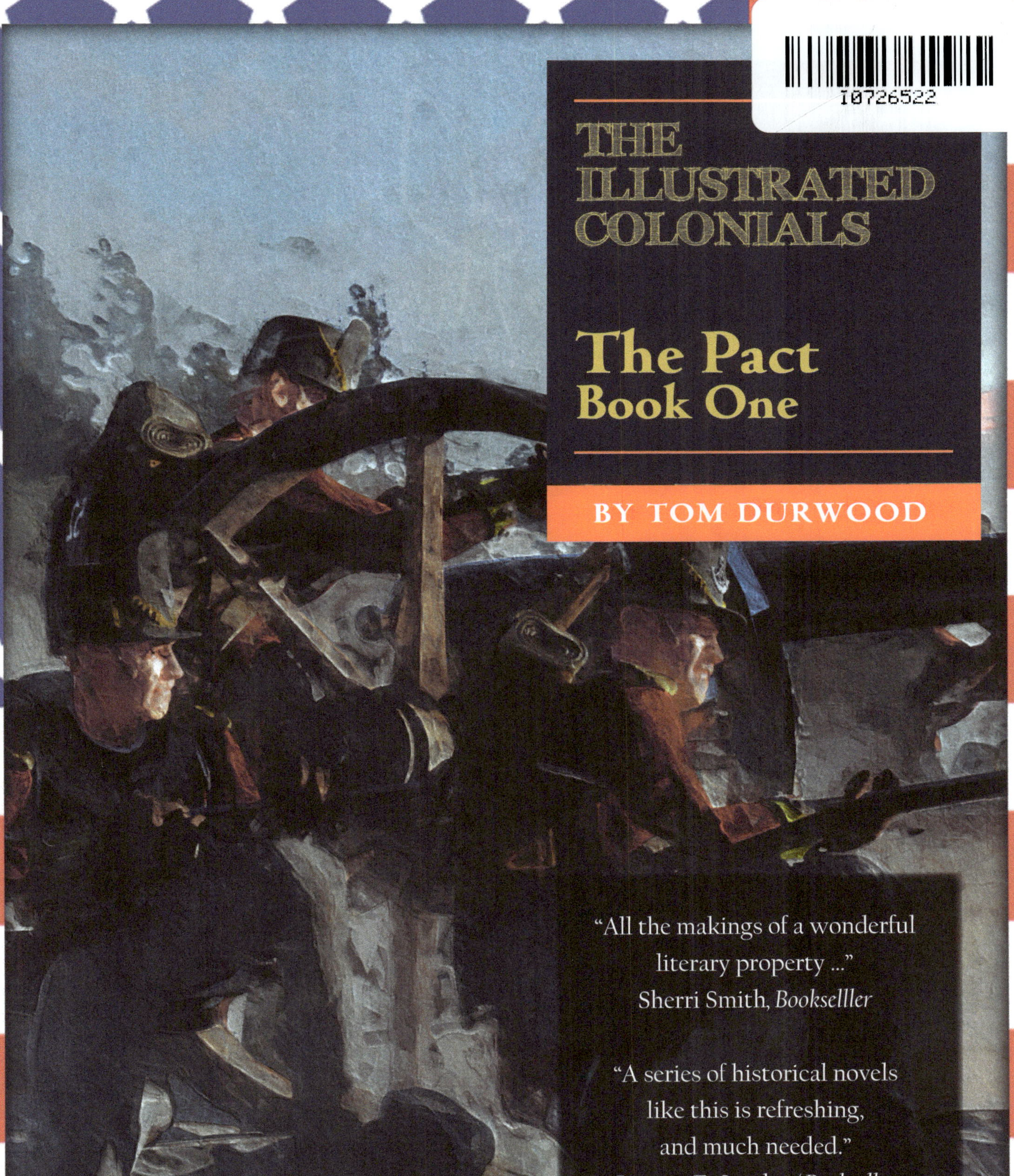
THE ILLUSTRATED COLONIALS

The Pact
Book One

BY TOM DURWOOD

"All the makings of a wonderful
literary property ..."
Sherri Smith, Booksellier

"A series of historical novels
like this is refreshing,
and much needed."
Lauren E. Snyder / Bookseller

I0726522

Foreword

FOR GENERATIONS, YOUNG AMERICANS HAVE been introduced to the Revolutionary War by Ether Forbes classic, *Johnny Tremain*. Penned in 1943, the novel features an apprentice who experiences personal hardship, forms a lasting bond with a friend, and finds fulfillment by joining the colonial resistance to Great Britain. It's a good story—as far as it goes.

In recent years, historians have broadened the selection of Revolutionary players and expanded the Revolution's stage. The cast now includes women, African Americans (enslaved and free), Native Americans, and colonials of all stripes. Further, the stage now stretches across the globe—challenges to the British Empire in Europe, Africa, and Asia, spurred by the Revolution unfolding in North America.

How can we introduce young readers to these new and expansive views of the American Revolution?

Thomas Durwood has found a way. In *The Colonials*, adopting but widening the *Johnny Tremain* template, he features six diverse protagonists who face adversity in curious ways, form lasting bonds with each other, and join the fight against Empire— not only the British Empire, but oppression in their own countries as well. The cast is diverse: Jaiyi Mei Ying from China, Prince Mahmoud from the Ottoman Empire (now Turkey), Sheyndil from Russia, Leo from Germany, Will O. from Holland, and Gilbert from France. Although each, in his or her way, is a misfit at home, they come together in common cause—a cause that will reshape the world.

At the unique "School for Young Monarchs" in the Alsace-Lorraine, these wayward youngsters, who push and pull and tease as teenagers do, are exposed to ideas of the Enlightenment—serious food for thought. Quick learners, they pick up innovative techniques of industry, agriculture, and commerce. They are also exposed to a political philosophy that is spreading among educated elites in Europe—and, better yet, taking root among all classes in America. There, disgruntled colonists are upset at being taxed without having any say in the matter. They insist that a government can rule only by "the consent of the governed"—a message that will resonate with oppressed people far and wide.

What can our crew of six do to support this worthy cause? That's where their adventures begin—in America and elsewhere. Readers, beware: you are in for a romp across the globe. The story is wild, but there's reason for this madness. Historically, youthful Americans have been presented with a limited view of our Revolutionary War, as if it were our business alone. But as this book suggests, powerful themes of the Declaration of Independence—liberty, equality, and "consent of the governed"—resonated throughout the world.

Fast forward a few years, when readers of *The Colonials* encounter histories of other nations in college or as adults. Foreign nations and cultures will not feel quite so "foreign" to them. They might or might not recall the particulars of Durwood's plot, but the characters will reside within them, as will the cause to which they had all pledged their allegiance.

—Ray Raphael, author of *People's History of the American Revolution*; *Founding Myths: Stories that Hide Our Patriotic Past*; *Founders: The People Who Brought You a Nation*, and seven other books on the Founding Era. Raphael is also an associate editor of *Journal of the American Revolution*.

YOUNG ADULT HISTORICAL FICTION
Early Readers' Comments

This is a surefire series. The nebulous Navigators are a key element, I think, since they provide a fantasy element and well as linking the stories. Does Cynthiana appear in the next one? I hope so.

I would publish *The Colonials* first. I think young readers will enjoy and recognize the academy for royals as pure Harry Potter. I'm glad you tie each of the royal teens back into the story (it's a clever plot).

At a time when history seems particularly vital and textbooks seem increasingly bland, **a series of historical novels like this is refreshing, and much-needed.** The series will do well with those already clamoring for another Dan Brown novel or the next installment from Alexander McCall Smith, but I believe it will also expand on those audiences, offering entertainment to those who are mostly nonfiction consumers, and a dose of history for those oriented toward straight mystery and thriller. **The timing couldn't be better for these substantive and entertaining novels.**

Lauren E. Snyder / Bookseller, Malaprop Books /Asheville North Carolina

This has all the makings of a wonderful literary property. It's like *The Da Vinci Code* meets *Kidnapped*. It also reminds me of the British series *Wolf Brother* (I'm not sure why). I know of at least half a dozen people, both adults and teens, I could sell your first book to right now (and interest them in the next one).

I firmly place the writing in *The Colonial* and *The Book Keep* with Steve Berry, Bernard Cornwell, A J Hartley, and even a little Dan Brown.Please keep me posted on the progress of these books; I look forward to selling them.

Sherri Smith / Park Road Books / Charlotte, North Carolina

It's a clever premise, to have teenaged heroes coming of age and changing history, aided by the mysterious Society of Navigators. It seems you could spin out an almost endless cycle of similarly colorful scenarios. The existence of a secret society adds a bit of mystery and darkness to the story.

This will certainly appeal to teens. While the writing may be challenging for some young adults, it is not any more so than J.K. Rowling, and not nearly as much as books like *Octavian Nothing*. **Teachers will love these books.** We have a number of teachers who frequent the store, and they are always looking for a good book they can use to supplement their lesson plans. I would recommend this series to anyone who likes Dan Brown, James Michener, Elizabeth Kostova or Patrick O'Brian.

Gina Glenn / Bookseller/Buyer / Malaprop Bookstore / Asheville, North Carolina

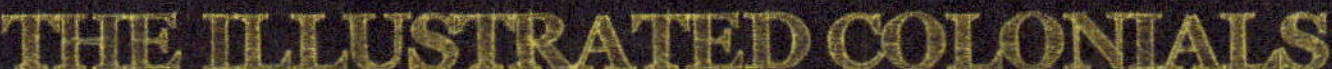

The PACT
Book One

BY TOM DURWOOD

ILLUSTRATED BY

Douglas Lobo
Timothee Mathon
Loronzo Natale
Mai Nguyen
Maria Cristina Pritelli
John Ramsey
Victorin Ripert
Jose Luis Segura
Jessica Taylor
Shahab Serwaty Nili
Karin Wittig
Sy Gardner

Published by the Empire Studies Press
www.empirestudies.com

ISBN The Illustrated Colonials Book One: The Pact   ebook 978-1-952520-14-3
ISBN The Illustrated Colonials Book One: The Pact   print 978-1-952520-15-0

Who shall write the history of the American Revolution?
Who can write it? Who shall ever be able to write it?

-- John Adams

Contents

Gallery of Main Characters

Leo
... An immature nobleman pressed to save his family's barony

Mahmoud
...Heir to a Sultan's throne, he now seeks a new destiny

Sheyndil
... Volga Basin seed collector thrust into treacherous times

Mei Ying
... strong-willed member of the Yunhe family, which operates China's Grand Canal

Will O.
... Boy savant who games the VOC to finance the Colonial cause

Gilbert
... A lost young romantic finds a cause worth fighting for

Prologue

SMOKE CURLED OVER THE BATTLEFIELD.

The Colonials had been overcome by superior manpower, superior artillery, and superior tactics.

The men of Boston had run out of bullets.

Now Major Alexander Lindsay, Sixth Earl of Balcarres, a tall, elegant man, walked the field at Breed's Hill with his lieutenants to exact a final price.

Fallen standards littered the red-scarred ground, scattered among the wounded soldiers. The air was filled with their moans.

There is such a thing as chivalry.

At Blenheim, John Churchill, the First Duke of Marlborough, captured his enemy, Marshal Tallard. Seeing that Tallard was wounded, the Duke offered up his own coach for the enemy commander's recuperation, while he (Churchill, that is) rejoined the fray.

There is such a thing as honorable conduct in war.

Saladin, at Jaffa, saw that his archenemy, Richard, fought with outstanding bravery, against terrible odds. When he saw Richard's horse get shot out from under him, Saladin sent two of his own horses, so that the Crusader could fight on, in a worthy manner.

There is indeed a tradition of civility on the battlefield.

But it did not extend here.

Not at Bunker Hill.

"For God's sake-- " begged a young patriot who lay on the ground, attempting to rise despite his wounds.

Balcarres jammed his bayonet in the boy's throat.

"This is *atrocity*-- " gasped another Colonial, an older man. "You'll pay, Balcarres-- '

"No," replied Balcarres as he emptied his pistol in the man's chest. "They'll blame it on the Cayuga--"

He handed the pistol to one of his lieutenants. He was given a freshly-loaded gun.

"These are farmers," said the Earl of Balcarres. "Citizen soldiers.

"They don't know how to fight. They think that their passion for their homeland will win the day."

"I call upon your *humanity*, sir," said a Colonial who had managed to sit up. "If not for me, then for the boys-- "

"But you *lost*," commented Balcarres as he shot the man in the face. "You lost the battle."

He reloaded the pistol, taking his time, relishing the ceremony of it. He took up a rifle and fixed the bayonet.

"We gave mercy to Monro at Fort Henry," called a young Continental whose leg had been shattered. He was a handsome youth, with burning eyes.

"Colonel Munro is not here," replied Balcarres briskly as he stuck the youth in the neck with a bayonet. He twisted the blade.

"The rest of the world watches," gurgled the boy.

"But the rest of the world prefers to watch. Not to participate."

Balcarres kicked the body away.

"This insurrection will dwindle quickly. Then disappear," the British officer pronounced to the small entourage walking with him across the field. "The rebels have no money. No training. No real army. No real Navy."

The unplanned engagement that had no name, the conflict that we call *The Battle of Bunker Hill* in retrospect, had been a one-sided affair. The rag-tag herd of patriot farmers had been annihilated by a professional army with strategic skill and disciplined purpose. This had not been a battle intended to wound a few enemy soldiers and so convince them to surrender and retreat. It was not a battle to influence the enemy, or a show of strength, or a battle for position. The British intended to kill every last colonial they possibly could. The faster they did so, the sooner they could quash the rebellion and return home.

"They write well, these Bostonians," said Balcarre. "But they do not know how to fight.

"And Lord North was so worried.

"We will soon own all of their farms. Their wives. Their cows."

"Who will save them?" smirked Balcarres.

The British officer repeated the question, as though he liked the sound of it.

"Who is it?"

He paused to cock and fire his pistol at another prostate wounded man.

"Who is it that the Colonials hope will come, to save them? Eh?

"*Who?*"

PART ONE

Call to Adventure

The War of Independence grew to be a world
war, with men fighting from Florida to Canada,
from the Caribbean to Africa to India, and across
broad reaches of high seas.

-- *Jon Meacham*

CHAPTER 1
The Power of An Idea

Men being, by nature, all free, equal, and independent,
no one can be out of this estate, can subjected to the political
power of another, without his own consent.

-- John Locke

THE FACE WAS VERY YOUNG, and very determined.

Freckles were sprinkled across the girl's nose and upper cheeks. Just sixteen, Jiayi Mei Ying took after her mother – reserved, willful, an aspect of red cheeks and swept-back black hair above a high collar.

The girl's eyes were clear, and smart, and took in all before her. A glimmer of fire flared in them when a passing vendor made her almost topple the laden tray she was carrying. Wariness around the edges of the eyes hinted that this was a girl who had seen more of life's darker side than most. The delicacy of her features was deceptive.

Floating far above, gulls called out, wondering what was in the boxes.

She turned the corner, balancing the tray in her two hands carefully.

The print shop of the Yunhe, in downtown Zhangzhou, overlooks that section of the canal where the channel widens to a lake ringed with wharfs to receive the traffic coming from the Xiamen ports, eastward, and the China Sea beyond, and the great Pacific and Indian oceans beyond that, to the interior.

The modest, red-shingled shop entrance sits on the slope among bustling cobblestone streets of tailors and vegetable stands, small merchants and big-wheeled peddler carts. Over the doorway a wooden sign swings in the breezes that rise from the open spaces above the broad canal, and the volumes of moving waters.

The bamboo door to the crowded, noisy print shop swung open.

Smiles appeared on the beleaguered faces of the printers when they saw Jiayi Mei Ying, youngest daughter of the Peiken family, the extended family whose members manage the all the waters, lands, and operations of the vast *Yunhe* Canal territories.

Mei Ying carried a black tray loaded with three heavy boxes.

She carefully removed the boxes from the black tray and placed them on the counter, careful to avoid woodblocks and racks of copper type.

The *dayinji*, or in this case the *zhiding dayinji*, of the Canal Territories, worked ceaselessly. Their presses chattered all day and all night. Consistent was the flow of printed information to disperse to the people and ships along China's greatest canal, a thousand-mile kingdom-within-a-kingdom.

Mei Ying called out her greeting.

Behind came her burly second cousin, Teng Sho, carrying a second black tray, also piled high with *jīng bājiàn* pastries.

Sweet fragrances rose from the distinctive red wrappings hiding still-warm cherry rose-bud puffs and caramelized rice cakes. Eight varieties in all. The sounds of whirring cylinders and clacking presses bounced off the walls and ceilings.

"Another pamphlet, eh?" commented Li Jie, the second shift supervisor with a smile.

"The best one yet," replied the girl.

The shop boys began to leave their posts and form a ring behind the chief, wiping hands on aprons. These particular pastries were only available from the bakers at Daoxiangcun, and few were the families who could enter that shop.

As the pastries began to disperse among the print boys, Mei Ying removed the pouch from over her shoulder. From the pouch, she removed a document.

She placed it carefully on the counter.

"We have two schedules to put out, for the line chiefs," said Li Jei, "then a dispatch for your Father. Then we can get to it."

He nodded to Mei Ying. "Thank you for the pastries."

She bowed extra low and extra long, for she knew she was asking for extra work, and paper, and ink, without any reward beyond the pastries.

"Thank you, *yin biao ji*," said the daughter of the Yunhe.

"It is well that we share the word." She used the term *minzhong*, which can mean 'beloved people,' but can also mean 'countryside of China' or 'worthy villages of China.'

Li Jie hefted the document, as though weighing the words and concepts it contained.

The document would have to go through the shop proofreaders to become a proper pamphlet, for Mei Ying, while enthusiastic about certain concepts, was no scholar. It took time and care to find which characters in the vast Chinese lexicon might best be used to correctly capture the meaning of phrases like "natural liberty" and "common sense" and "taxation without representation."

The ideas ... would soon shiver the nations, known and unknown, present and future.

Mei Ying took her leave.

The door slapped the frame behind her, leaving the print-shop steward to look through the pamphlet she had left behind. It had a green cover, as unassuming as any accountant's chart, but the ideas within it would soon shiver the nations, known and unknown, present and future.

* * *

"The consent of the governed."

The young woman, a teacher, had risen to her feet without being noticed by the Magistrate or his aides. She gripped a much-read green pamphlet in one hand.

When she spoke, the words snapped in the air, clear and firm.

"Madame?" asked the Magistrate.

These meetings with the peasant class usually went smoothly, with the *fumu guan* reciting newly revised laws, a charter, and schedules of 'donated' labor.

"You can only pass such a law as this with the consent of the governed," said the teacher.

The Magistrate, a tall, aloof man with an officious manner, looked blankly at the speaker. She was no more than a girl.

He conferred with an associate.

"You refer to the crazy *waiguo ren* ideas," he ventured.

"The Prefect makes good use of *waiguo ren* cavalry when he sees fit," came the teacher's retort.

"This isn't *Hebei*, you know," the assistant reminded her. "This isn't Shanxi—or *Boston* -- "

She waved the green pamphlet in her hand.

"The Qianlong Emperor acts in the interests of the people," the teacher stated.

"You have said so yourself. Many times."

"Yes. It is widely known," the Magistrate replied.

"Well, this is not in my interest.

"The burden of this labor on my family is too great. My family will starve if my two brothers are conscripted for this long a time. As with the fathers of my students.

"We do not consent to build the Emperor's road to Zhangzhou!"

"Young lady, the Governor canno-- "

"*Mark me,*" she warned, interrupting.

She shook her head.

"We have not consented."

She pursed her lips. She put her hands on her hips.

"You cannot govern us."

* * *

"*Get back in line or sink!*" called Jiayi Mei Ying.

The voice through the megaphone was high in pitch, rich with menace. The words were slow and distinguishable, for all the ships in the queue to hear.

"Back in line, *Long Shou* -- "

On this bright morning, a mid-sized sea hawk from the Anhau Province kept trying to butt in line at the very entrance to the Canal.

A trio of skitter boats chased it, their leaders narrating on the megaphone. The brightly colored flags on the small quick vessels gave an unmistakable message.

The sea hawk *Long Shou* defied all these commands. She darted among the grain barges and military transports.

Twenty-two boats patiently obeyed the queue, and watched the interloper, waving him off.

The tillerman of a four-oared tax collecting vessel stood and shook his fists. The crewmen of the grain barges looked on with amusement: no one jumps in line on the Grand Canal. The *Yunhe* see to that.

Members of a brace of cormorants who nested at the Canal, patrolling the waters with their shaggy crests, looking for food, squawked at the commotion and looked on, curious.

"*Last warning ...*" called the voice through the bullhorn.

A curt burst of a cannon exploded from the lead skitter's deck and the *Long Shou's* mast blew into bits.

Birds scattered.

A second cannon fired and fishing nets splayed over the *Long Shou's* deck, catching man and canvas and tiller in its chaotic sprawl. Panicked shouts and cries erupted from the deck.

Three quick detonations from the skitters and chained grappling hooks shot out and hooked onto the *Long Shou's* gunwales.

The skitters abruptly came about and, sails straining, began to ferry the disabled sea hawk out of line, to the docks.

Once the ship was grounded, the pilot charged down the wharf, arms flailing wildly, screaming threats and insults --

Striding towards him at the same speed was Jiayi Mei Ying, the teenaged girl who had ordered their capture. Three youths her own age trailed close behind.

"You do NOT impede the Anhui War Lord," shrieked the pilot, a well-dressed young man in his early twenties. His manner was that of one used to getting his own way.

"I am LAO BAN!" he screamed. "My father is the Commander of the Cloud Cavalry! Oh YES!"

"*Feng gou!*" came the low warning from one of the trio with the girl.

"You will REPAIR my *boat!*" shrieked Lao Ban.

At ten paces, Jiayi Mei Ying flung what looked like a block of wood at Lao Ban.

The block of wood separated into two; the twin blocks were connected by a rope.

"You will LICK the VARNISH as I watch your PATHETIC – *urk!*"

The rope struck the young noble in the neck and wrapped around his throat, so that the two stout blocks of wood slammed him in the head.

He crumpled and fell to the dock.

"I am Jiayi Mei Ying," she told the crew of the now-unconscious Lao Ban.

"I am unranked in your system. But my family runs this Canal, on behalf of the Emperor. On behalf of the people.

"You have broken the rules of these waters. Now you will pay the price."

Mei Ying bade them pick up their unconscious pilot and join her family for lunch, before they began their sentencing, and then the repairs.

* * *

"I'm not sure I CARE," announced Mei Ying, in a tone of disrespect that could not be mistaken, "WHAT the third of the three great hydraulic engineering projects of the Qin Dynasty might be."

"*That's it,*" replied her Grandfather, Ting Wen.

"You're out."

The old man spoke assertively, clearly, wanting his voice to be heard all across the classroom.

It had been a long morning. Miss Lo had guided her students in drawing detailed pattern maps of the effects of flash flooding in sedimentary gullies and gorges. It is not a topic that can be covered quickly, or summarized, or short-cut in any way. Engrossed in the details of the alluvial fans of the Koszeg mountains, Miss Lo had skipped the students' 10:00 tea break.

Hence Mei Ying's outburst.

Now, she and her classmates (many of them her cousins) looked around at one another.

Even the teacher, Miss Lo, seemed taken aback.

Ting Wen was a village elder, and he often sat along the side of the classroom, beneath the windows, rarely speaking until the instructor's lesson ended and tutoring began.

"*What?*" demanded Mei Ying.

"Get out."

The old man indicated the door, using a nod of the head, as you would to an old friend, who knew what you meant anyway.

Mei Ying rose form her desk angrily, making sure to generate clatter and chair-scraping sounds as she did.

"All right," the student said loudly. "I WILL get out, then -- "

"You're on your own now," replied her Grandfather. "Good luck."

Jiayi Mei Ying tore open the door in an effort to draw attention away from the tears beginning to well up in her eyes, and her shaking hands.

She slammed the door shut behind her.

So began the journeys of China's legendary Navigator, greatest of the modern era.

CHAPTER 2

Gilbert

The racket made by the American rebels
woke citizens in the sleepiest corners of
the civilized world.

-- Sally Schildhauer , A Brief History of the Navigators

JEAN FRESTEL, THE DRAGOON, BLOCKED a sword-blade and parried. His young opponent was a swordsman only in the crudest sense, in that he wielded a bladed weapon. Beyond that ...

Whack! Parry!

"Ow! That hurt -- "

The boy grabbed his hand with a bitter curse, dropping the sword.

Frestel had come three days' journey from Paris to rouse his moody young friend, Gilbert du Motier, only to find the front door barred.

"Madame Paulette!"he called to the tall polished-wood doors at the entrance of the manor at Chavaniac estate.

"Please unlock the doors!"

Gilbert's grandmother was within.

Now two of the guard-boys lunged clumsily at Frestel at the same moment. Their blades clattered against one another.

Frestel parried, refraining from slashing back, for these were kitchen-boys and farm hands, dressed as guards.

"It is Jean Frestel – Gilbert's friend from the Regiment -- "

"Yes! I remember you-- " said the voice on the door's other side.

"No one has heard from Gilbert since our discharge. Is he alive?"

"Scarcely, I dare say – thank God you are here -- "

"If you can just open the door -- "

"Yet I am prevented from opening the doors!" said the grandmother from within. "Gilbert gave strict instructions. You see my quandary ... "

The Dragoon noticed the big windows along the manor's eastern flank and leapt onto the ledge.

The windows shut with a slam.

He cursed and called his friend by name and many rude nicknames.

He reached to his left, among the climbing ivy –

Where was it?

He knew that the original architect had built a ladder into the flanking walls, so that for maintenance of the repair the manor's roofs.

Frestel pulled himself up.

The Dragoon peered through the glass. He could see no one in the chambers there ...

A noise drew his attention upward –

A female face appeared --

The attic! Of course!

A secret door had led to a hide-away at the very top of the Chavaniac Manor.

His window was wide open. Frestel swung in and stood to regard his young friend and Dragoon disciple.

"Gilbert!"

A startlingly handsome youth, no more than 16 or 17 tried and failed to rouse himself from the bed.

Empty wine and liquor bottles lay among trays and baskets and plates of half-eaten food. A general air of debauchery and self-pity hung in the air.

Frestel chased way the two young women in attendance. "Get dressed!" he commanded.

Frestel grabbed Gilbert by the collar of his robe.

Young Gilbert 's blood-shot eyes avoided his friend's gaze. A black mane of tousled curls fell over the collar of his robe,

"You're coming with me," Frestel informed his friend.

"Where are we going?"

"Alsace. To help a man build a canal. An honest day's work won't hurt you –

"Besides. A hive of monarchists may soon descend on him. It might be dangerous."

Gilbert looked up --

CHAPTER 3

Shay

Catherine desperately wanted the German settlers
to fill the Volga Basin, and would do anything to get them.
She felt sure that farmers would save the Republic.

-- *Saul Dubinsky, A Brief History of Botany*
The Volga River Basin, west of Moscow

"TAKE A MOMENT. *SEE* WHAT you're doing."

The girl Sheyndil called to the mules, both individually (by name) and as a pair, as she struggled to properly till the rich black-earth fields.

She was unused to the new metal plow. She fought to keep it steady in the rows. She had in her mind how she wanted the field to look. She wrapped cloth around her blistered hand as she called encouragement to the mules. Gradually she taught herself how to balance these new plows, in motion, in conjunction with the steady forward force, and the pace set by the animals.

It was past lunchtime when she finally led the mules to the barn to unhitch the plow, and to fetch grain and water for the animals. She apologized to them for yelling at them.

She entered the longhouse.

"*Svolach*," said the matron. "Let me see that hand, girl ..."

The longhouse was busy with activity, Women opened barrels of rice and tea and stirred bog cauldrons

of stews and tended ovens. Against one wall rose a bank of wooden shelves lined with glass and ceramic. jars. The jars had labels with names like amaranth, cherry, coriander, Brandywine, heirloom, rainbow, Virginia ...

"Shay, come and see what the coachman brought us," said Sheyndil's little sister. She was perched on a ladder in front of a large map. The map was decorated with brightly colored ribbons and pins. "Dwarf wheats. They don't bend in a storm, apparently ..."

"Hey!" cried Sheyndil. "Don't throw away the papers-- "

"Why not? It's just stuffing-- "

"No, the Virginians -- this isn't stuffing! It's his – his correspondence.

Thomas always does that."

Just then, a commotion of horses and wheels and drivers came from the western doors. The doors facing the road from the north- west. The road from Moscow.

"Who is it?"

The carriages stopped.

Uniformed men opened he carriage doors and pointed to the longhouse.

Sister waved at the visitors.

"I – I don't know – some *Russkayas*-- "

Two women made their way along the dirt path through the fields. One was wearing a wig and formal dress. As they advanced, behind them men were raising tents. No hide-and-bone contraptions, nor yurt nor *yaranga*, but a French-style pavilion, with high pointed canopies.

"Ah. Hullo," said the one in the formal dress.

"Let me," began the woman. "I am-- it is I, your -- oh, Clotilde, would you -- "

The second woman stepped forward.

"May I present Sophie Friederike Auguste, Prinzessin von Anhalt-Zerbst, Grand Duchess Yekaterina Velikaya."

She paused.

"Catherine. Empress of All Russia."

"I have come to speak to the young Jewess," said Catherine the Great.

"The farm girl. The seed girl. Shay."

"I am Sheyndil," said the girl.

"Ah! Well met," said Catherine. "I expected you to be thickly built. And mannish. But you're not at all. You're very pretty."

The two Moscow women entered the longhouse, stepping sideways .

"My dear," said the Empress Catherine. "Ah. What a lovely house ."

She smoothed her petticoats.

"I wondered if, on my behalf, you might take a trip. A voyage."

Catherine smiled warmly at Shay.

"Twelve hundred miles. Westward. To Europe."

Sheyndil closed the fingers of her bandage-wrapped hand.

She opened and flexed the fingers of that one hand, then the fingers of both hands.

Ah," said Empress Catherine. "Shelves and shelves of seeds, I see..."

The fires crackled and popped.

"We might discuss your trip, over lunch. In my pavilion."

The Empress sounded hopeful.

"I wondered if, on my behalf, you might take a trip. A voyage." Catherine smiled warmly.

CHAPTER 4

Leo

As America cracked open traditional models of government,
tensions and rivalries rose among the German states.

-- Sally Schildhauer, A History of the Navigators

"Good people," began Udo, Leo's father.

One of the hot chestnuts in the half-dozen fireplaces of the Lodge Hall popped.

Udo smiled, and pretended to duck. He had been drinking all evening, so he stumbled slightly.

It was a tradition for the people of Thedinghausen to celebrate Walpurgis Night with the Lord of the Margraviate.

Udo Krummensee-Grabmaler, Heir to the House of Hohenzollern, Lesser Magistrate of the Margraviate of Brandenburg, raised his mug of mead and addressed the restless crowd. His daughter and son stood at his side. His face was flushed.

"Good people. Friends! Another harvest has come! To good fortune!"

Yet the Barony of Ehrbhof had fallen upon hard times.

"Fortune does *not* smile on us, *Sire*," complained Melton, the village activist.

"Lombard has dammed up our river," he continued. "We can walk the dry river bed. No boats to bring sheep in, or to take our wool to market. Our Schweiz neighbors encroach on our lands --

"The wolves hunt our oxen while your son practices crossbow on squirrels ..." said another villager.

"*Lord Ugo.*" One of the villagers stepped forward, a burly man in farmer's clothing. "Disease plagues us. We have no doctor. We sent word to Leiden. For all we know it's a blight, and our children will be next. Can you not help us?"

"My dear woman, we-- " Ugo held out a hand in a show of sympathy.

"A council was held last month, in Stuttgart. German unification. Did we send a delegate?" demanded Herr Melton.

"That could change our fortunes! It was only two days from here."

Others joined in, voicing concerns from bandits on the eastern roads to the mill taxes.

"You can't just give speeches!" called a woman's voice. "You have to *govern.*"

Udo squinted in concentration as he listened to the complaints. He handed his mug to his son, Leo, to be refilled. His daughter, Romy, urged him to sit down.

Lord Ugo Udo Krummensee-Grabmaler, Heir to the House of Hohenzollern, Lesser Magistrate of the Margraviate of Brandenburg, banged loudly on the table.

"Well spoken, brothers!" said Udo, raising his glass to make a toast. "Sisters!"

"To all! Our hopes and wishes!"

* * *

Afterwards, Leo's cousin, Luc, a Hohenzollern on the Prussian side, spoke privately to him and Romy.

"Herr Melton is circulating a petition. This could be disastrous. You could lose your title, lose your estates. It specifically calls for you two to be cut off from all sponsorship. You would be penniless.

"What should we do?" Romy, two years older than her brother,

Luc, a merchant in his mid-twenties, cautioned them. "It would be better if you were both out of sight, Your presence seems to enrage Melton and the others-- "

"Werner has asked me to marry him -- " offered Romy.

"Leo," said Luc, "an acquaintance of mine knows of an estate just across the divide, in Alsace. Selestat. They run a select school for such as we. You could spend a season there, out of sight, until things calm down … "

CHAPTER 5

Mahmoud

The American nation was born as
the centerpiece of an international coalition.

-- Larrie D. Ferreiro

"HE LOVES THAT JACKET, DOESN'T HE?"

The Harbor Mistress, Cynthiana, looked down from the Topkapi palace tower on the lawn, where Mahmoud, wearing his red and blue celestial jacket played sword with his brothers.

"It's time," she told Bayazid, their mother, who stood beside her.

"Already?" Bayazid twisted the silk scarf in her hands. "Are you sure?"

"He is a clever, well-meaning, spoiled, roly-poly Prince," said the Harbor Mistress. "He has logged no time in the real world, nor met an idea that challenged him."

"This school in France," said Bayazid. "It worries me so. He has never been away from home so long."

"We send him to live among the infidels," said Bayazid. She was the Sultan's sixth and most influential wife.

"Europeans are the nicest of infidels," replied her friend, the Harbor Mistress. "I hear there will be a Dutch merchant prince. And an apprentice of Catherine the Gre -- there! Is that the new wife?"

"Yes. She's very young, they say ... "

Cynthiana turned from the window.

"We must help Mahmoud become the man he is meant to be. He will be Sultan one day."

The tides were in. The *Sehsuvar* sailed at noon.

CHAPTER 6
Will O.

I wanted movement and not
a calm course of existence.

-- Tolstoy

July, 1775, Amsterdam, The Netherlands

"How CAN you?" exclaimed Johannes.

Close-up, sitting at the chessboard, Will looked impossibly young. Wide-eyed, impressionable, sandy hair, hazel eyes, Will favored his mother's side, in looks and demeanor – slim, stoic, light-haired, quiet (to a fault). His older brother Caspar was louder and more social, like their father.

"How can you cut him out of the family business?"

Let us say that it all – the whole adventure, really – started at the moment the Oldenbarnevelt boy was denied his rightful place in this world.

"You might as well *disinherit* him!"

Will's godfather, the shipping agent Johannes Sykes, paced back and forth before the parents, irate, as they dined.

Will sat at a chessboard in an alcove by the window of the dining room, with its dramatic black-and-white floor tiles and its tapestries and mantled fireplaces.

The family cat sat opposite Will.

Will made the Bishop Sacrifice on the cat's turn.

The sprawling Oldenbarnevelt home made much of patterns of light. Slanted sunbeams were everywhere – on the black-and-white checkerboard tiled floors of the kitchens, resting softly on the wooden roof beams, cutting diagonals on the patterned rugs, glowing on the cream-colored porcelain plates adorning the high shelves, sparking prisms of color in the goblets of stippled glass. Hand-painted fabric designs from India and the Orient hung on the wall. Outside, visible through the tall windows, ships moved on the stately canals of Amsterdam.

"That is exactly the OPPOSITE of what you should be doing-- "

"Primogeniture." replied the father, Pietr Oldenbarnevelt. "It's not exactly a new practice, Johannes. The first-born gets everything."

"Primogeniture." replied the father. "It's not exactly a new practice, Johannes."

He was a formal man, smart but not brave, aware of traditions, sensitive to society's opinions.

"And you approve of this?" demanded Johannes Mickler of the round-faced woman at the other end of the well-set table.

Madame O. nodded as she finished chewing a mouthful of roast beef.

"But Will is smarter than Caspar," argued Mickler. "No offense," he added, with a nod to Caspar, the tall, elegant older brother, who stood beside Father's chair.

"None taken," said Caspar.

"Caspar is socially adept," said Mother. "He is well-liked. Will is painfully shy."

"Will is a hard worker," said Mickler. "I have told you how helpful he was with the *Intrepid*'s ledgers."

"He spends too much time among the ships and the sea-men," said Mother. "Too little among the people who count."

"Caspar is the older brother," pronounced Father, ending the discussion.

"Caspar inherits.

"He will have lawyers and bankers to advise him. Two brothers, two owners would never do."

"Then," said Johannes, "if you are to banish your younger son from the family business, may I suggest that you grant him a lesser route, or two? The Bosporus, for instance."

"Give him a trade route, you mean? To Bosporus?" asked Caspar.

"Aye," said Mickler. "The Baltic, the Hebrides – they are of little value, yet they may allow him to earn a living. Unless you want an indigent son wandering the alleys of Amsterdam."

"Very well," said Father. "I agree to that."

"And have you made inquiries into that French school, Johannes -- ?" asked Mother.

"Aye. Will and I depart for Marseilles Saturday. We meet the Chinese girl."

The servants collected the dishes. Kind Beatrice set out an extra slice of pie for Will.

"All very well," said Caspar. "All good."

Father sipped a glass of sherry, which he believed helped his digestion. Caspar downed his in a single gulp.

Will moved, Knight to Pawn 2, knowing he had surprised his feline opponent.

The cat paused in her grooming to look at the boy across from her with a combination of superiority and disinterest.

"Kingside pawn rush," Will told her.

PART TWO

School

Let those who have abundance remember
that they are surrounded with thorns...
-- *John Calvin*

CHAPTER 7

The School for Young Monarchs

There are three ways by which a nation might acquire wealth.
The first is by War; this is Robbery.
The second is by Commerce, which is generally Cheating.
The third is by Agriculture, the only Honest way.

-- Benjamin Franklin

ON WILL'S SECOND DAY, GILBERT reached to grab Will's backpack --

"Don't touch him," snarled Mei Ying.

Leo and Gilbert and Mahmet (a nickname for the more formal 'Mahmoud') and the Russian girl, Sheyndil, turned and looked at Jiayi Mei Ying.

"I think I *will* touch him," said Gilbert. He snatched the backpack and shoved Will rudely.

Will fell to the ground.

He scrambled to his feet, fists raised.

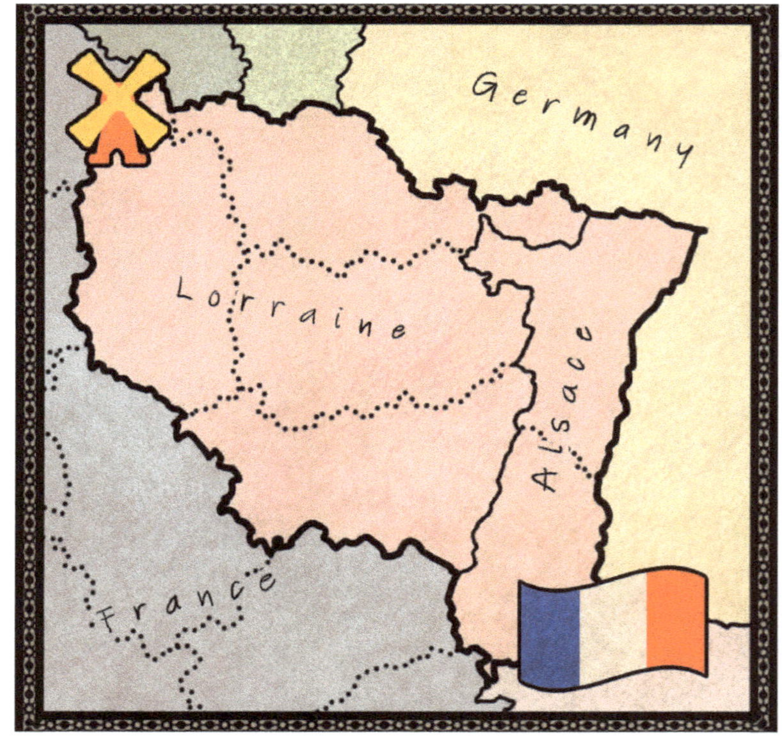

But Gilbert, Gilbert Marie Jean Paul Joseph Roche Yves Gilbert du Motier, Chevalier of the Noailles Dragoons, heir to one of France's largest fortunes, among the eldest and most respected of students, lay splayed on his back, on the ground, eyes wide, nose bleeding.

Mei Ying had kicked him with a sort of round-house motion of her leg and foot – too quick for the eye to see -- and now she stood over him, still, ready.

"Try it again," she said.

Leo gave a low whistle. Sheyndil clapped her hands.

"You must show me how to do that!" said Gilbert, laughing, first in French, then in English, then Mahmoud repeated the phrase, also laughing, in Arabic.

* * *

It didn't look like a school.

The Navigators' compound at *Nid de Corbeau* in the hills of Alsace, above the village Selestat, looked like a cross between a working farm, a zoo, and a monastery. There were a series of barns and barn-yards and livestock corrals on the left, a main house at the center, and a stone lodge with a stout tower which seemed to extend forever on the far right, at the juncture of a small stand of trees and a rock outcropping, connected to a set of crags. Benches and tables were arranged under shade trees and along cobbled paths through the grounds. A stream came from the orchards at the property's northern frontier, across the fields where sheep grazed, down through the extensive gardens, and under the stone mill that dominated the central compound. Some diverse group of remarkable architects had left their marks: great wooden stilts buttressed a sort of tree-house wrapped around a trio of small stone structures that might have been left over from the Roman era; a series of rope bridges connected trees and treehouses; here and there a Moroccan window design and a Chinese roof gave hints of the ancient and worldly sources from which sprang the *Nid de Corbeau* compound.

A camel walked past.

A family of giraffes foraged methodically in the crown of a shady oak tree.

Two peacocks followed the camel, at a distance.

* * *

"Where is Teng Sho?" asked Mahmoud with delight.

Mei Ying's cousin and protector was rarely seen, yet when needed he unfailingly appeared, on the instant. During those times when he chose to linger, he was a friendly fellow, willing to trade stories. His skills with languages were equal to Mei Ying's.

"Why are we speaking English?" asked Mei Ying.

"*Souvent Francais aussi*," answered Sheyndil.

"We speak *English* out of respect for the *Colonials*," answered Leo.

"The Bostonians," added Mahmoud.

"The Continentals," said Leo.

"We admire their cause, and intend to help them," said Sheyndil.

"You all have different answers to the same question," remarked Mei Ying.

"That's the way it should be," said Gilbert.

As they walked around the yard towards the kitchens, Will complimented Mahmoud on the bright red star-patterned coat he wore.

"He thinks it makes him look warriorly," said Leo.

"It reminds me of home," corrected Mahmoud. "It is a birthday gift. From my father. The Caliph."

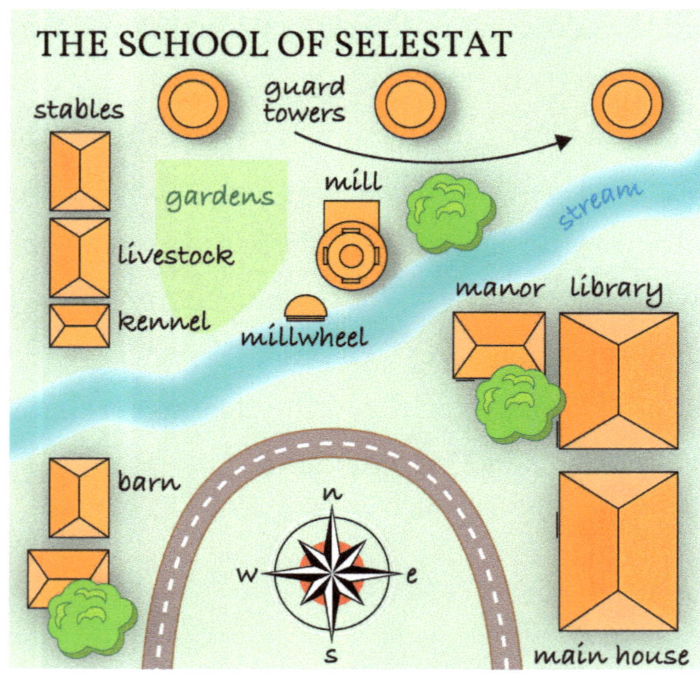

* * *

"Shay. Please name what the British think are the Nine Rules of War," Master Frestel requested.

"I cannot, sir."

Leo raised his hand. Frestel ignored him.

"Mei Ying!" continued the Master. "Name the Nine Rules, won't you, then apply two of the rules to a battle."

Leo waved his hand to and fro in desperation.

"Show me how well you understand them," Frestel directed Mei Ying.

"Force is Rule One ..." she began.

"No!" cried Leo.

"And *Leadership* is Rule Two -- " she continued.

"Wrong!" Leo was hopping up and down in his seat. "She means 'Unity of Command,' and it's not *Two*, it's *Six*-- "

"Very well. Leo, apply it to a battle."

"That's easy. At Crecy, the French broke rules five, seven and eight-- "

"This isn't fair!" protested Mei Ying. "The boys raise their hands even when they don't know the answer. You can't let him recite-- "

"You had your chance, Madame Yunhe," replied Frestel. "You were just making things up -- "

"It's still not fair-- "

"Protest all you want," said Master Frestel calmly. "I don't care if you hate me. You will each emerge from this class knowing how to write a solid five-paragraph essay, on any topic, whether you enjoy it or not.

"After this recitation, you will all be composing a clearly argued, fully grammatical essay of three hundred words, in which you will each pick two new rules, and two new battles.

"And if I do not care for your answer, you will be doing Miss Ayen-Noialles' barn duty."

"What?" exclaimed one of the Asfour brothers. "Why does she get special treatment?"

"Because I like her more than I like you," explained Frestel.

Leo gave his two battle examples.

Even before he was finished, the scratchy sound of pens on paper filled the classroom.

Frestel hummed while he paced.

Soon, he would interrupt them to glean their progress, and to outline their essays as a group.

You will each emerge from this class knowing how to write a solid five-paragraph essay, on any topic ...

They did listen to one another. They were fascinated by one another.

He stopped at the window.

Outside, in the pens, he saw that the new boar was kicking up a ruckus. He apparently intended to have all the sows for himself. He was a surprisingly mean-spirited creature.

* * *

"Decimus," asked Sheyndil one night. "Where might I find Nitidus?"

She was respectful enough to use the gladiator nicknames which Leo and Mahmoud had given themselves that week.

"Nitidus is right there," replied Decimus (that is, Leo), indicating a fortress of pillows and blankets which occupied the far side of the dormitory room. The structure had been arranged to block off all human contact. Blankets had been draped to act as a roof, so that its occupant could stare silently out of the structure's sole portal, which face the window.

"What, is he practicing the Sultanic signature?" asked Sheyndil.

"No. He is just in one of his black moods," explained Decimus (Leo).

"Oh. Can he hear me?"

"I don't see why not."

"Nitidus," she said to the wall of blankets and pillows.

"Master Dubin just told me that I spend too much time in the library. I told him that I am only here for the seeds. But apparently, I am required to attend all the classes.

"These stupid battles. He says if I don't pass the exams this week, I'm out -- "

"He told Gilbert the same thing," said Will.

"Mahmoud, I wondered if you might consider tutoring me and Gilbert," said Sheyndil. "You seem to remember everything that is said in class.

"It is the Battle of Lutzen. Gilbert is convinced that Adolphus was leading the Holy Roman Empire, and I am quite sure it is Wallenstein. I'm afraid we are hopelessly lost."

There was a long silence.

"I suppose I could," came a voice, somewhat muffled but nonetheless distinct.

* * *

To complete the Canal, a mix of hands had descended on the private lands of the *Nid de Corbeau*, above the French village of Selestat, in Alsace, bordering the German states. The Scots Navigator had sent three sturdy shipyard workers to lend support to Master Dubin, first among equals in the Society of Navigators, and his student helpers. The formidable African Navigator, Umukulo, had arrived with his niece. The Asfour brothers, from Egypt. Now Frestel and his moody friend, Gilbert, had joined, and the Dutch boy, and the rising leader of the *Yunhe*, the girl Mei Ying, with her escort, Teng Sho ...

The Canal was almost complete. After decades of clearing the old Roman canal and poking around the quarry and making designs, Dubin had been inspired by Daffyds, who had successfully built an eight-lock canal in the wild hills of Wales.

And by the Colonials.

When he read Jefferson's phrase, 'life, liberty and the pursuit of happiness,' Dubin understood it as a personal mandate. He knew how badly the villages of Alsace all sought connection to one another, connection over the hills, like parts of a family long divided. It was in his power to connect them, especially now that Daffyds had shown the way ... to help them pursue happiness. Such was a government's duty, and the government was made of citizens like him.

The wheeled carts which transported the giant blocks through the forest were of Egyptian design, from the diaries of Ib'n Bin Said, from the days of the Pharaohs.

Many were the days Dubin had spent staring at the terrain, drawing its features, shapes and degrees, guessing at the geologic layers he could not see. He had to speculate as to how the water would react (always a surprise). He was endlessly adapting the design to the specific slope, for even the sandbox builder knows that details must always hold true to the whole.

The Canal's seven locks served as receptacles, or basins, you might say, for the waters that would soon rise and fall up and down those rocky slopes like a giant set of steps, a most valued waterway, since the alternative was the slow-moving Saar, little brother to the Thur, some 120 miles to the south. The Selestat Canal would essentially create a shortcut, a new and direct tributary crossing into the Rhine valley, perhaps a more accurate replica of the river's ancient pattern.

From Jalmari's stacks they culled sketches of wooden lock-gates, found in Leonardo's *Codex Atlanticus.* From the Swedish shipyards of the Twelfth century came the designs for the narrow pencil-shaped boats that would run the canal, narrow enough so that one could fit in each direction at the same time.

Students served as apprentices on the stone carving and steam-bending of wood beams, learning all the secrets of the canal-designer and shipyard worker ...

In the staging area, just above the canal walls, where the two cranes loomed, Leo, Mahmoud worked hard.

They carved and smoothed the second-to-last of the great stone blocks so that it would fit snugly into the canal's great rock steps, needing as little concrete grout filling as possible. Dubin had a sharp eye for it.

"You're WEAK!" gloated Leo as Mahmoud faltered. They had been working all morning.

"You are Athenian, lost in ideas," he continued.

"I am Spartan! I never complain!"

"Yes, I love SCIENCE!" replied the Ottoman Prince. "And DEMOCRACY!"

He set down his mallet for an adze.

"The girls are better workers than both of you. All three of you," called Dubin from his station, two locks down the slope, including Gilbert in his assessment.

"They work *smart*."

Shay was fitting shards and slivers of rock between the plates while Mei tapped them tight with a boucharde,

Just then, Umukoru and two of the Cossacks appeared over the rise with the final block, swaying from a crane.

"The girls are better workers than both of you. All three of you," called Dubin. "They work *smart*."

"Those wolves grow bolder by the day," muttered Umokoru.

"Are you sure this is how Leonardo did it?" asked Will plaintively from down the slope, where he struggled with assembling the wickets for the miter gates.

Dubin turned his attention to wickets.

CHAPTER 8
School Scenes

But there it is. One word
used up already. Blue.

-- Howard Moss

"CANAL WORK IN THE MORNING, cooking and gardening and barnyard chores in the afternoon, then class, dinner and study," said Will, standing at the sinks, towel in hand, at kitchen duty.

"I can't even hold my arms up..."

He stepped off the stool for a moment.

"Go and sleep, Dutchman" said Sheyndil. "I can finish these -- "

Will stepped back up, redoubling his efforts.

"By God!" whined Leo. "How can one man eat so much?" Gilbert had just brought in a stack of plates left by the African Navigator.

"Umukoru is as strong as any three of us," replied Mahmoud. "He practically built the southern wall by himself. No wonder he's hungry."

"He's built square," said Leo. "I wouldn't want to meet *him* on the battlefield."

"Frestel could beat him," challenged Mahmoud.

"Never bet against Frestel," said Gilbert.

Before more could be said on the topic, Mei Ying came through the doors carrying a stack of plates.

"Look to," called Sheyndil with a laugh.

Mei Ying slid the dishes into the big sinks with a great splashing, to Leo's noisy protests --

"Being part of this group," said Will, "I feel I can do anything.

"I have decided that this is what it's like to have a real family," he added.

Mei Ying and Shay nodded in agreement.

"How does all this water get here without buckets?" asked Leo, as if just noticing.

"Pipes," answered Mei Ying, pointing to the copper tubing along the wall.

"Plumbing. There is a water tower on the roof. Gravity does most of the labor -- "

Leo looked at the Yunhe girl blankly.

"I'll take you on the roof tomorrow" said Mei Ying. laughing. "You should know how such things work."

Both Mahmoud and Sheyndil said, 'Yes, we'd like that.' Leo, not wanting to be left out, chimed in.

* * *

"You're so conceited," whispered Shay to the blonde mare, Tessa.

The young horse nodded her head in agreement, making sure her mane shook out prettily in the morning sun.

"You are the most beautiful creature," confided Sheyndil.

She held the carrot in the flat of her palm.

Tessa leaned over and took the carrot, munching with big crunching sounds, noticing how the Russian girl admired her, even as she ate. Tessa was pregnant with her first colt, and felt that she deserved special attention, even more so than usual.

"But not too beautiful to help me with the plow."

Sheyndil tossed the halter on the mare's neck and missed.

The mare snickered and cantered off to join her comrades in the meadow, as Shay cursed in Russian --

* * *

The library tower at the *Nid de Corbeau* compound was built into a tree-shrouded grove abutting a cliffside, so that looking at the modest entrance, it was impossible to tell how far the interior chambers reached. Similarly, sitting in one of the front reading rooms, the depth of shelves and stacks which stretched and curled into the back could not be seen. Standing at any one point, in the library at *Nid de Corbeau*, you could see only one wall.

A tall, silent woman stood almost hidden among the stacks, casting a protective eye.

"Her name is Jalmari," said Mahmoud. "She's always here."

"I heard Dubin call her *Jara* once," said Mei Ying.

"I think her husband was a Navigator," said Mahmoud. "Helsinki."

"She is wonderful. She knows everything." said Sheyndil. "We correspond. We trade seeds."

"She doesn't seem wonderful to me," said Leo.

The cavernous archives, its sloped roofs, punctuated by tall windows and shafts of light, were organized by continent. Often, when a student arrived at the library, they would find a stack of folders with their name on it.

"Is that why you're here?" Mahmoud asked Shay. "Seeds?"

"They say the Empress Catherine herself sent you," said Leo.

"Aye."

"What for?"

"She covets the German farmers. In the Volga Basin. And they listen to me.

"At least, she thinks they do.

"The Volga farmers will look favorably if I bring back better seeds. And the light plows. And plans for canals, like Dubin's. And aqueducts. Russia needs everything. We're not like France."

The soft sounds of papers shuffling and ink pens on parchment took over.

"I heard Gilbert has fought the Spaniards. He and Frestel," said Leo. He was designing a tree-based combat trap for use on a forested battlefield.

"I heard the King has prevented Gilbert from leaving the country," said Mahmoud. "Is that true?"

They all looked at the Ottoman Prince.

* * *

"Come, *solnyshko*," beckoned Gilbert in Sheyndil's direction as she entered the near barn, by the row of sinks.

"Stand by me. Here is the soap. You look like a peasant -- "

"I *am* a peasant!" exclaimed Sheyndil, stopping at the sink next to Mahmoud, shoving him over one.

"Is that true?" asked Leo. "Are you?"

"No, she's not-- " Will sputtered. "That's *ridiculous* -- "

"She is a natural royal," said Gilbert. "She and Mei Ying are the most royal among us..."

"There's no such things as a 'natural royal' -- " said Will.

"I don't own any serfs, if that's what you mean," said Shay.

"That doesn't make you a peasant," said Leo.

Gilbert snorted.

"I work with the land," added Sheyndil. "There is dirt under my fingernails..."

"So does Master Dubin, and he is no peasant," said Will. He snatched a towel angrily. But the question seemed to bother him.

"All this talk!" he concluded. "We're *all* royal! Isn't that the whole point-- " He reeled off a lengthy curse, in Walloon, and then another in low Dutch, so that no one could follow, but he was careful to fold the towel and hang it properly before stalking off.

"You're staring," said Mei Ling to Gilbert when they were alone, as they dried their hands.

"At Sheyndil. You can't do that."

"Do what?"

A row of white ceramic sinks dominated the sizeable mud room of the fist barn. Mei Ying hung the hand-towel on its rack.

"She takes your attentions to heart.

"She's has no defenses against someone like you.

"Besides. Her people will need her."

"You don't know that," said Gilbert.

"Just as your people need you, Jeel-bear," countered Mei Ying.

The young Frenchman snorted and started to reply, but a pair of monkeys chased across the rafters above and they had to duck their heads.

Outside, a quarter moon was appearing in the evening sky, too early, so that it could only be seen in contour, and only if you knew to look, and only if you looked directly at it.

CHAPTER 9
Never Two Without Three

None are more hopelessly enslaved
than those who falsely believe they are free.

-- Goethe

"Didn't you read the Hobbes chapter?" Mahmoud asked Leo.

"I can't," said Leo.

Mahmoud turned to look at his friend.

"I can read the words," continued Leo. "I just can't – I stare and stare, but I can't – I can't really pull together what they mean, you see.

"I'm useless," he added.

"Just as well. I shall go home and make sure Romy's set. Then I'll join the Twelfth Regiment."

"Hessians?" asked Mahmoud. Leo nodded.

The six of them were grouped around the fireplace, amid rugs and blankets in the manor's third-story living room.

"I'm sure your family needs your help in running the Barony -- " Mahmoud told Leo, setting aside the pamphlet in his hand. "My father, the Sultan, numbers the days until I can rule by his side -- "

"I have friends in the Twelfth," replied Leo. "I'm good with guns."

Sheyndil picked up the book.

"*From this equality of ability ariseth equality of hope,*" began Sheyndil, "*in the attaining of our ends...*"

Reading Hobbes is something to be shared, anyway ...

* * *

A curious young giraffe stuck its head through the tall open windows of the dining hall.

"The Colonials falter," said Dubin as the plates were being cleared. "The early promise of Brandywine and Bunker Hill is gone. The British have the odds now."

"Don't count them out just yet," said Umukoru. "Those Virginians will stay the course.

"And the Iroquois. The Five Nations could shift the tide. It's their war, too."

"If France doesn't join in soon," said Frestel, "with all their ships, to distract King George, I don't know how Washington can survive the Winter."

"The Hudson may be the key to the war," said Master Dubin.

"A river like that ... if only Washington would drop everything else and seize the Hudson Valley, it would allow him free movement north and south. Anyone who looks at a map can see that. I can guarantee you that Burgoyne sees it-- "

"Every week – every day – spent training the farmers who call themselves soldiers will win battles," added Frestel. "Without training, they are surely doomed ..."

The giraffe moved its neck in a slow swivel, turned its attentions to the bowls of fruit.

"You youngsters have been born into momentous times," said Dubin to the students who sat listening at the adjacent benches and table.

"The Bostonians have triggered a world war. Nothing less. Everything is about to change, in ways none of us can predict.

"Each of you is a member of a family with a wide reach.

"Each of you has enemies, some openly declared, some pretending to be your friends. You will add to that list if you champion these new principles.

"Liberty. Equality. Pursuit of happiness. These are beautiful ideas, truly.

"But we must all keep in the front of our minds the wreckage they can bring. Leaders among the Colonials have lost their fortunes, had their family member shot and killed, been chased from their homes.

"Your folk need to understand these new ideas. You are their hope. You must bring these ideas home, and in doing so find your own destinies.

"Beware. Much is asked. The price is always high. Higher than you think."

* * *

Standing at the kitchen stoves, Shay was humming. It was a folk tune, one of the calendar songs, comparing the seasons. She had a big spatula in one hand.

"What is that?" Mei Ying asked the Dutch boy.

Shay and Will and Mei Ying had breakfast duty.

"Will, why are you doing that?"

There was no answer.

The young Dutchman was moving the eggs from space to space in the cupped carton, in a continuous motion, faster and faster, twice switching the entire carton end to end. It was a practiced protocol. Mei Ying stopped her bacon-frying to watch as Will's hands and fingers moved faster, chasing some shifting pattern, or the shadow of a pattern, that only he could see.

"They have to be arranged just right," Shay told Mei Ying. "He does it three times."

When the eggs were lined up in the carton, just so, the dexterous young Dutchman held up one.

"Ah. Now we're ready -- " said Shay.

He handed the egg to Sheyndil. Whatever sequence or progression Will had been following, it was now complete.

Humming, Shay put the spatula down. She cracked the first egg crisply on the cusp of the bowl, then put her hand out for another.

Mei Ying nodded.

It went quickly after that, and soon three steaming platters overflowing with scrambled eggs with shallots and baby tomatoes and a pinch of cheese, every platter ringed with bacon and the spicy sausages that Master Dubin favored, were set out on the galley tables.

* * *

"Who is your favorite colonial?" Mahmet asked one evening, in their rooms.

"Adams," replied Mei Ying. "He writes with great passion."

"Jefferson," answered Shay. "He is a farmer."

"Von Steuben!" answered Leo. "He is more of a soldier than any dozen others. He knows a formation or two."

"Franklin," said Mahmet. "He has wit."

"Washington is the greatest of all the Colonials," said Gilbert. "Without him, there is no American cause."

"There may not be an American cause anyway," said Mahmet grimly. "They are out of money, and their ships are blocked from foreign ports."

"Huh," chuffed Leo. "Washington is full of himself. He means to be the American King, just you wait ..."

CHAPTER 10

Encounter in the Village Square

Those who had squandered their free will
were ... ripe for enslavement.

-- *Simon Schaama*

"Mahmet, you enjoy eating."

Sheyndil smiled.

"Come and smell the lentils," she said. "Pick the ones you like -- "

The morning outing to the village square started innocently.

They were in the village market early that morning to set up booths for our fruits and vegetables – the *Nid de Corbeau* produce was widely admired. Villagers visited the long stall beneath the banner of a crow's head in a circle. Music played in the square, where children danced.

Sheyndil picked up a handful of the flageolet beans. She wore a blue scarf at her neck, a distinctive Russian blue. She rolled the white beans through her fingers. Mahmoud and Leo stood watching her.

They had ridden in a wagon down the twisting road from the compound to buy and sell food, to visit the village shops, to collect mail, and to buy candy, and to mingle among the commoners. Frestel had an order to pick up at the printer's. Mei Ying and her protector preferred not to be seen in public.

"Are these not unusual?" laughed Sheyndil as the Ottoman Prince and the young German baron cautiously inspected the legumes. "See how thin-skinned the blonde lentils are."

"It is true that I enjoy good food," replied Mahmoud Mustafa Hasan Husameddin Cezayrili, third son of the sixth wife of Sultan Abdulhamid, Caliph of all Muslims, Secular Ruler of All the Ottoman Empire.

"I like to eat," said Mahmoud. "But I do not *cook*. Peasants cook." At this, Leo Krummensee-Grabmaler, Heir to the House of Hohenzollern, Lesser Baron of the Margraviate of Brandenburg, snickered.

"We agreed to call them 'citizens,'" corrected Sheyndil.

"Very well," said Mahmoud. "The citizens who act as my servants enjoy cooking for me. They have told me so on countless occasions."

"*How stupid are you?*" demanded Gilbert, who stood nearby.

This outburst surprised them. The moody Gilbert so rarely addressed his fellow students directly.

"They don't enjoy cooking for you, any more than they enjoy washing your dirty clothes or shoeing the dirty hooves of the horse you ride or shoveling snow from your path so that you do not get wet feet. They don't even *like* you," Gilbert continued loudly, warming to the topic.

Sheyndil hurriedly paid for the lentils and ushered the group away from the stalls and out into the cobbled streets.

"They don't *respect* you. Amongst themselves, they laugh at the spoiled brat who could not even earn a single day's pay for honest labor."

"Do they?" asked Will. "Do they really laugh at us, Jeelbare?"

Will combed his fingers through his hair. It was a sign of concern.

"How do you know?"

Gilbert smirked and shook his head.

"Anyone who has a *monetary* relationship with you ... cannot be believed," he told Will. "If you or your family in any way benefits them, then *of course* they will always laugh at your jokes, and agree with your every opinion, and come promptly when you are aggrieved. But falsely so. Always falsely so. Tell them you have no money. Tell them you have lost all your money gambling, and that your family needs lots of food, and a place to stay. Then you may see how deep their devotion is."

"Do they?" asked Will. "Do they really laugh at us, Jeelbare?" This idea seemed to upset him.

"Jeelbare, why are you so upset?" asked Shay. "Did your letter from America not arrive?"

"No! It didn't! But that is beside the point. If we are ever to amount to anything, any of us, we must shed these ridiculous shackles of affluence. That is the point of everything that is happening. Can you not see that?"

The Turkish Prince was about to lend his opinion when suddenly two riders on horseback appeared in a great show of snorting and clatter, right in front of the five students, blocking their way.

The two men were collectors, in the employ of the local lord. Swords hung from their saddles. Their steeds were black-maned Friesians, horses whose scarred hides gave proof of past battles: these were warhorses, beasts as might once have pulled a chariot, and they strained at their riders' reins, eager to charge into the students' midst.

"We are thirsty," declared one of the riders gruffly. The bright yellow and red crossed-keys-with crown patch marked them as monarchists in the employ of Michel Ovando, the landholder and investor recently down from Paris, titled Lord of the neighboring estates, staunch supporter of the King.

"We require a tribute," stated the first rider.

Leo, who longed for battle, turned, his eyes growing wide.

"You lot look flush enough-- " said the second.

"*Beware, thou rustic. Thou calumniator!*" warned Leo in imprecise French.

"You're Brandenburg," said one of them to Leo. "You're safe. For now. Where is the new one?" he scanned our ranks. "Where is the Dutch lad -- "

His eyes found Will.

"Ah. The Oriental girl must be nearby -- "

Leo unsheathed a dagger and rushed at them --

The second rider knocked Leo to the ground without removing his leg from the stirrups.

"Ugh!" Leo splayed on the ground, his knife clattering.

"Give me that-- " The first rider snatched Sheyndil's bag from her arm.

"*You can't--* " she protested.

"Yes, I can. I might take you as well, Princess-- "

Gilbert stepped forward, hand on hilt.

"I am of the King's Dragoons," said he, inserting a common gerund between the word 'king' and the word 'dragoons' to indicate that he was there to give battle.

"Ah, yes, the Nursery-School Regiment. I have heard of it," chuckled the first rider. "You must be out on maneuvers this morning. Great dangers lurk among the fruit stalls. Come a bit closer, *Dragoon--* "

A shadow fell sharply across the lane. The riders looked up, squinting.

"*There is easier prey this morning, gentlemen ...*" said a low, threatening voice.

A tall man had stepped into the alleyway, inserting himself between the riders and the students. His broad sword blade flashed shiny and ready, in the sunlight, held at a most willing angle outside the man's cloak.

"*... Elsewhere than here.*"

It was their chaperone, Master Jean Frestel, a man who had fought for the throne at Ramillies and Malplaquet, and in the Wars of Austrian Succession. In his left hand, he held a flintlock pistol, aimed squarely at the lead rider.

The Ovando rider paused.

"You wouldn't shoot me-- "

"Let's find out," growled Frestel.

He cocked the pistol's flint, making a heavy click.

Leo snatched Sheyndil's bag from the second rider's gloved hand and hissed at the black horse, who started, confused by the sound.

The two riders glared, then thought better of it.

They moved on.

"Look to your school, young ones," warned the first rider darkly. "You may soon receive visitors."

Master Frestel guided the group quickly towards their wagon.

"Did you hear that accent?" the schoolmaster asked aloud. "Hungarians."

"Ho, I look to the day we meet again, thou Hungarians! Thou brigands! *Aaagh!*" Leo called back to the departing horsemen, although he was now speaking in German.

"Oh JESUS of NAZARETH. Let me *go* and I will carve them like -- ACHILLES *ABSENT* is ACHILLES *STILL!* Do you hear me?"

He continued, inexplicably, in flawed Latin, to the effect that the noble blood in his and his friends' veins traced back to Caesar, or at least the days of Caesar.

"What's wrong?" Mahmoud asked Sheyndil, who had gone pale. "What is it?"

"I saw one of Tyomkins' men," she answered. "In the crowd."

"Who is Tyomkin?"

"Catherine's Minister of Agriculture, and a man who bears me only evil. It cannot be an accident that he is here."

"Maybe they are just visiting the countryside," offered Mahmoud, after a while, but no one believed it.

Soon Leo's well-crafted shouts became lost in the clopping of the horses' hooves on wood, as the wagon crossed the bridge over the river Allier.

"Any?" Will asked, of Gilbert. "Not *any* of our servants love us? Are you sure of that, Jeelbare?"

But Gilbert was done speaking for the day, so Mahmoud took up an explanation of the case for equality in the great brotherhood of man as the wagon rolled through the late morning sunlight. His pleasant voice and encouraging words hovered over the little group as they moved bravely, uncertainly, up the curling road, and into the green foothills of Alsace, above the village of Selestat, towards *Nid de Corbeau.*

CHAPTER 11

A Neighbor Visits

After Bunker Hill, landed gentry everywhere began
to glance nervously at their house-servants.

-- Saul Dubinsky, A Brief History of Botany

"THERE WAS AN ENCOUNTER," SAID the visitor.

"In the village square. Our men acted like barbarians. I am so sorry."

Mme. Ovando, mistress of the neighboring estate, stood at the front entryway to *Nid de Corbeau* manor. She was a short, stout woman with a pleasing voice and a warm smile.

"We have come to apologize to your ... students. A thousand thousand apologies," she bowed, turning to Shay and Leo, who was tall and handsome.

"It is the strain of these troubled times."

Mme. Dubin stepped forward to greet her neighbor and assured her visitor that all was forgiven, and that it was nice to meet at last.

"You may know my husband," said the visitor. "Michel Ovando, and my youngest son Pierre -- "

Lord Ovando was a tawny, tousle-haired man, big at the shoulders. The son wore a hunter's jacket, belted at the waist. He was one of the horsemen from the village.

"We are recently down from Paris, and have neglected to introduce ourselves. You must come for dinner."

"We have come bearing gifts!" Mme. Ovando clapped her hands.

A serving girl appeared from the small entourage, bearing a heavy silver tray mounted by a large cake, decorated with a thick frosting. She was petite, and wore a blue patterned dress with a white apron, and her face was partially covered by a crow of blonde hair.

"Thank you!" exclaimed Mme. Dubin. "You must have spent hours over the ovens, my dear -- "

The girl smiled shyly.

The silver platter slipped for a moment.

Mei Ying, standing next to the servant girl, caught the plate before it could tilt --

With a low curse, Pierre Ovando raised his hand to cuff the family maid –

Suddenly his legs were swept from under him --

No sooner did he hit the ground than Will and Gilbert were leaning down to help the nobleman to his feet.

"I'm afraid the cobblestone is still wet," Gilbert apologized. "We mopped just this morning."

"My!" exclaimed Mme Ovando, pointing towards the path. "So the stories are true!"

All heads turned to see two of the giraffes sauntering towards the orchards, where they preferred to spend the mornings, before visiting the pond for a cool drink. A chatter of monkeys could be heard from the near barns.

"People send us exotic animals they bring home from abroad," explained Mme. Ovando. "They would otherwise be abandoned ..."

The monkeys lined up along the near barn roof to look on, placid for now.

"Might we see your *library*?" sked Mme. Ovando innocently.

She began walking toward the library tower --

"I've heard so many good things -- "

"I'm so sorry."

Frestel blocked her way, in no uncertain manner.

"Our librarian is doing inventory." Frestel's manner was as icy as his voice.

"She does not suffer interruptions."

"Really, young sir, we seek only a glimpse -- " said Mme. Ovando in a most reasonable manner.

"She is adamant," said Gilbert, stepping next to Frestel.

Mme. Ovando looked around, patting her hair, which was pulled back in a fashionable bun.

"Well, Another time, perhaps. Hah! A camel! Wonderful -- "

She shook hands warmly with Mme. Dubin and said it was good to finally meet, and that they would arrange a longer visit.

The dark look which Pierre Ovando gave Frestel suggested it might not be arranged for some time.

CHAPTER 12

Recitations

The aristocracy has not survived this long
due to its intransigence.

-- Julian Fellowes

MEI YING ASKED GILBERT, IN French, if the clay had effectively sealed the pipes where they joined, so that no water leaked out.

"*Bin- ha*," responded Gilbert.

He had learned a clutch of Chinese phrases from Teng Sho, whom Gilbert admired.

They were on the library roof, trying to replicate an impressive plumbing array of water pipes and chutes which Mei Ying had seen in one of the archive journals, regarding Rome's provinces. The Roman Emperors Caracalla and Diocletian had apparently pleased (and thereby controlled) their subjects by providing plentiful water in colossal baths, dams and reservoirs, drains, spas, heated floors and home faucets – contributions Mei Ying thought would be popular among her own people.

Mei Ying seemed to take Gilbert's answer as satisfactory, for she added two more copper pipes to the framing.

When she was done, Mei Ying yelled for Leo to turn on the valve leading from the water tower (three barrels roped together, connected by wood chutes).

He did so.

The pipe sections burst apart, spraying us all in a torrent of water.

Sheyndil swore in earnest at Mei Ying.

"Look!" said Mei Ying. "If the block-headed -- " the adjective she used was harsher "— *Romans* can build it, so can we!"

"I see the problem!" called Gilbert.

Hearty sounds of clanking and pounding on metal rose in the Alsacian sky above the library.

* * *

"He's off me," said Shay during a break from the reading. It was John Locke, and that is heavy going.

"Just as well."

"Who is?" asked Will carefully. "Jeel-beart ...?"

Sheyndil stretched her arms and rolled her neck, stiff from a full day of work, first on the Canal, then in the barns.

"He scarcely looks at me."

Will glanced at Mei Ying, who made no response.

"Wear more of those dresses with patterns, Shay," suggested Leo, not looking up from the drawing he was making (it was a schematic drawing of a large, winged weapon). "You look so nice in those."

Mei Ying smiled. A soft chuckle came from the corner where Teng Sho had stationed himself.

"Thank you, Leo," said Sheyndil.

She picked up the book.

"The end of law," she read, "is not to abolish or restrain, but to preserve and enlarge freedom -- "

"How can you 'enlarge freedom'?" asked Leo. "It's already pretty large, I'd say ... "

"Shush, Leo," said Shay. She continued reading.

* * *

In the stables, seeing Mei Ying struggle to lift the barrow high enough to dump the grain into the feed troughs, Mahmoud dropped his broom to come to her aid. Half of the grain spilled out on the side of the barrow, forcing them to scrape it up by hand.

"I can't stand this," said Mahmoud with a depth of feeling.

"What?" asked Leo. "Cleaning the barn?"

"Physical labor of any kind," replied the Ottoman Prince. "Look, I'm *sweating* -- "

"You like food too much," Leo suggested to Mahmoud.

"Labor is no longer to be looked down upon," quoted Gilbert cynically. "It is the fulcrum to a better world. So say the Colonials."

"But we do so much *work*," continued Mahmoud, "it's a *joke* -- "

"I enjoy the library. And all the weapons," said Will. "And the Masters' stories. And we learned that leg sweep from Mei Ying, Gilbert certainly did -- "

Now, as Mahmoud lifted the barrow again, it swerved on its unsteady wheeled axis. It pitched and clattered to the ground. In his haste to sweep up the grain a second time, the young Ottoman let his broom handle hit the stall's partition behind him, causing the entire rack of metal bridles to clatter noisily to the stone floor.

"Gracefully done, O Sultan," said Leo, who had been watching, and then he added a Latin witticism (as he had heard the prefects do):

"*Factum non verbum.*"

"Do you even know what that means?" asked an irritated Mahmoud.

"Yes. It is a Roman adage concerning fat people trying to hide their clumsy mistakes."

"No. You just said, '*Deeds over words.*' It makes no sense."

"Well, peasants won't know what I'm saying, will they?, so it should sound most impressive to them when I am Baron -- "

"*You're the peasant*," said Mahmoud. "You don't know the first thing about – about anything -- "

"Take that back, Turkish *slug* -- ugh! There! Let that show you -- "

Leo and Mahmoud set to sword-fighting with their brooms, with Will joining in, and Mahmoud narrating in rapid-fire Anatole Turk. The monkeys gathered to watch, unsure if this fraternal combat was in earnest.

Gilbert rapped his awl on the wooden top of the tack chest to remind the group of work undone.

The students returned to their work. Master Dubin would be there to inspect the stables in less than an hour, and he would use a white glove if he suspected they had slacked off.

Mahmoud complained that he had a headache. Leo said he was thirsty, and that it must almost be lunchtime.

"I can stay," said Will. "I can finish."

* * *

One of the ewes, a sturdy mother of two lambs, was braying loudly because her lamb had gotten a leg tangled in the wire fence marking the chicken coops. Murmuring to calm the sheep, Will patiently detached the foreleg. She stepped free and trotted to her family, then turned to regard her rescuer.

Will was humming and sweeping the hay into neat geometrical patterns when he felt a sudden blow to his back.

What--?

The pain was unbearable. He doubled over and fell to the floor.

Who--?

A large, angry pig had butted him.

"Help!" called Will. *"Who opened the gate -- "*

Someone had left the pig pen open.

Will was struck again as he struggled to stand.

He dropped – hard this time –

He fell to his knees.

Now several pigs rushed towards him, panicked by some unseen commotion --

"Stop!"

He felt them tearing at him –

One hand on his stomach, another clutching the wood rail of the pens, he stood –

Now a brown boar came into view, different from the rest – a huge, wild-eyed beast with a nasty temperament. Confused by Will's presence and appearance, suspecting all rivals, the boar pounced --

"*Fight back,*" came a voice. "They'll kill you."

Confused by the change of space, the pigs turned frenzied.

Will reached for a rake hanging on the wall hooks. If only he could get that in his hands --

He was knocked down by grunting snouts --

He was dragged across the barn by a mob of snorting hooved beasts. He stood, only to fall into the muck-filled troughs --

If he could only open the gate to the back pastures …

His trousers and shirt were covered in mud and filth.

Will lunged and grasped the round metal lid of one of the horse-feed buckets.

Using it as a shield, he slammed it against the boar.

The barn monkeys, who fear all violence, exploded in protest.

Again and again, he smashed the shield against the oncoming hoard.

He struck out savagely until he had made room enough to dive under the pen's wooden fence.

He flipped open the gate.

One of the herd's dominant sheep stepped between Will and the pigs, bleating loudly.

The pigs re-routed.

The squealing mob was released into the fenced pastures.

It was the mother ewe Will had helped earlier. She waited until he was safe.
The wild boar looked at Will. He blinked. He trotted off.

* * *

"Citrus acts as a tonic," recited Sheyndil. "The acidity of the oranges neutralizes the toxins."

She waited for signs that the others had learned and understood.

"Come now. What neutralizes a toxin? Say it."

"Do we have to?" whined Leo.

"Yes," replied Shay. "Dubin will ask it on the test tomorrow."

"Citrus and quinine," said Mei Ying.

"Oranges and lemons," said Mahmoud. "Citrus and quinine."

"So we should all carry grapefruits with us," said Gilbert, from the chair where he sat polishing a dagger. "In case we are poisoned."

"One of my uncles was poisoned," volunteered Mei Ying. "Arsenic. It was awful."

"By whom?" asked Shay.

"A mistress," answered Mei Ying. "While he was sleeping. This was back, a year before my banishment ... "

"You were *banished*?" asked Gilbert.

"Aye," replied Mei Ying evenly. "I was. By the Emperor. I killed one of his nephews."

"He deserved it," she added.

These two statements, taken together, produced a long, complex hush, a sort of charged silence in which change was occurring, change at an accelerated pace, as though some air-borne alchemy was rearranging the warm atoms of the atmosphere. Everyone was thinking.

"And how did you kill him?" Leo asked Mei Ying at length.

"If I told you, you wouldn't like me anymore," replied Mei Ying

"Oh, that's all right," said Will. "We already don't like you-- "

The Dutch boy pounced on the daughter of the *Yunhe* --

Teng Sho tensed and then relaxed, hearing her laugh, for Will alone among them could touch Mei Ying, much less wrestle her to the ground and mock-batter her.

CHAPTER 13

A Brace of Villains

You see the bodies. You smell the smoke.
But the larger picture eludes you.

-- Kurt Wimmer

CHUGUNOV, TALL AND WIRY, LEADER among Tyomkin's agents, cut to the chase.

"What is it exactly, Madame Ovando, that you propose?"

The time for preliminary discussion was over.

She waited for the servant girl to retreat.

The parlor door closed behind her.

"I propose an expeditionary force to visit our mysterious neighbors," answered Mme. Ovando.

"A raid. An unfortunate and cataclysmic fire on the main grounds."

"To what end?" asked Chugunov.

"We each have different ends," came the reply.

It had been a pleasant get-together up until now. The parlor of the Ovando estate was most handsome, and the food unusually thoughtful.

"My interest is the Jewess," said Chugunov. "Commisioner Pugashev is a patriot. Catherine takes Russia in a dangerous direction. These new seeds, these new methods of agriculture -- "

"It would be best all around if the Jewess does not return to the Volga," he concluded. "If she dies in a fire, on a farm in Alsace, no fingers will point in Pugsahev's direction."

"As to our participation," said the refined Niu Hsing, in excellent French, "it ends with this delightful tea."

He placed his cup in its saucer for emphasis.

"Among the Chinese, the *Yunhe* are honored. Legendary are the generations saved by the *Yunhe*'s leadership in times past. They have saved entire provinces during flood and famine. One does not take arms against any member of the *Yunhe*, whether in Peking, Paris, or the farthest moon of Jupiter.

"So we take our leave. Thank you for the cake."

"My interest," said Mme. Ovando, when the Chinese delegation had left, "*our* interest, our family's interest, is in the *Nid de Corbeau* property. Our lawyers have discovered a flaw in the title. If we can postulate illegal activities, we have a chance at overturning the deed. And taking ownership."

"I assume the canal," said Chugunov, "figures largely in your plans. I understand it is almost completed."

"The library," replied Mme. Ovando. "The gardens. The orchards. It is a most ... unique property. Unique and varied."

"We have heard rumors that there are treasure maps woven into the rugs in that library," said Chugunov. "Alchemists' secrets. Celestial charts going back to Charlemagne. A collection of books and charts and magical knowledge to rival Alexandria ..."

His hostess made no answer.

The Russian shrugged his shoulders.

CHAPTER 14
Witches' Chants

I intend to go in harm's way.

-- John Paul Jones

THEY WERE SWIMMING IN THE mill pond, beneath the mill wheel when Sheyndil's skirts got caught.

The original mill at the school had been expanded to add stables. Oaken posts three feet in diameter had been buried to support a heavy roof over a row of stalls, several of them triple-height (for the giraffes). Fences had been constructed between the livestock and the cogwheels so their curiosity could not lead them to get caught in the great axle, or iron spindle, or the gearing. A Flemish braking system controlled the wheel's speed, a curved band of wood with heavy horizontal beams hinged to the wall. With each turn of the mill wheel, a brake lever lifted free of its catch, allowing the flow of water between the stanchions.

A favorite game among the older students was to dive beneath the mill wheel, which had been in the built in the French medieval style, embedded in the stone wall of the mill, half-inside and half outside; so that a clever swimmer could dive in, go under the wheel as it spun, grab tight hold of a shelf, and rise with it on the other side.

Sheyndil had been chatting with Gilbert and had not paid attention to the flow of water. She misjudged its speed, and when she dove in and sank out of sight, there was no corresponding shout from the other side.

It took a moment for this register.

Mahmoud noticed it first. He cried out her name. On the instant, following the urgency in Mahmoud's cry, Gilbert and Leo dove in. Mahmoud (slower, for his girth) and Mei Ying and Will all dove in to save Sheyndil.

Gilbert emerged with the half-drowned princess.

He lay her down on the hay of the mill floor.

They kneeled around her, watching her dripping, coughing form as she regained her breathing.

Will prayed.

Mahmoud emerged from within the mill.

Unexpectedly, he had gone clear under the millwheel and into the building.

* * *

Late that night, five of them crouched in the garden rows, in the creaking south windmill's shadow, under the bright moonlight.

Sheyndil sat on a bench overlooking the fenced pasture and played a folk melody softly on a pipe instrument, a sort of small-scale accordion. A herd of cows had gathered to listen.

"What are we doing here?" hissed Leo, who had only followed the others out of habit.

"The deer ate twenty head of cabbage last night," replied Sheyndil. "They must be reminded who owns this garden."

"Isn't this what the dogs are for?" asked Gilbert.

"Why don't we just shoot them?" asked Leo.

"Don't be stupid," said Sheyndil. "Without the deer, we would be overrun with-- "

"God in Heaven!" Gilbert let loose a string of curses. "Who could care about the damn cabbages but you?"

"Go back to bed, *chasseur*," said Sheyndil.

Several sets of glowing eyes became visible in the moon-shadows beneath the nearby stand of trees. The deer, stood at the edge of the rows, just under the alders, watching this unusual night scene.

"There they are! *Sortez! Allez-vous!* AAAGGGHHH!"

Sheyndil threw a clod of dirt at the deer.

"*J'en ai marre!*" she called out, making it personal. "*Tu me fatigues!*"

Unexpectedly, the Duchess d'Ayen-Noialles, just turned thirteen, suddenly stood and recited, with gestures, the entire witches' chants from the fourth scene of *Macbeth*. But it was not until her rendition of the verse with the *ravin'd salt-sea sharks* and *baboons' blood* that the deer seemed truly concerned, and bolted away.

"Huh!" called the French girl. "Come back tomorrow night for more, *vermin--* "

As they walked back along the mill path, Shay detoured to visit the mare Tessa, whom she spoiled.

A figure emerged from the orchards.

Will thought it was some sort of vision at first.

In the silver-and-azure patterned light, a small person took shape. Her slim form and blonde curls were unmistakable. He recognized the face and form of the Ovando servant girl, the one who had baked (and almost dropped) the cake.

She walked towards Will.

"You're the one who tripped Master Pierre," she said in broken French.

"I wanted to thank you."

"Th-- they are brutes, b-b-brutes, to ever raise a hand like that," said Will, struggling mightily against his shyness.

"I also came to warn you," she said gravely, one hand on Will's sleeve. She was close enough for him to notice bruises around one of her eyes.

"They mean to do you harm -- "

Will turned to see if perhaps Shay or Mahmoud could join him --

Then she was gone.

"Wait," called the Dutch boy. "What – what-- "

"Beware!" her voice floated through the orchard.

CHAPTER 15

School Life

Happy, thrice happy shall they be ... who have
performed the meanest office in erecting this
stupendous fabrick of Freedom.

-- George Washington

RETURNING FROM THE CANAL WORKS late one morning. Leo and Mahmoud saw Master Umokuru, the African Navigator, his distinctive face and figure well-hidden in the shadows of a thick line of birch overlooking a shallow canyon, descending from the border fences along the estate's western frontier.

He was watching a clearing, through which a path had been made by wild animals. Umokuru saw them. He bade them walk silently and sit behind him.

Together they watched. Their patience was eventually rewarded when a trio of wolves stepped silently into the clearing. They were headed south, towards the *Nid de Corbeau* livestock.

Umokuru put a blowgun – a thin, hollow reed of light wood – to his lips and puffed out three darts, so that his cheeks blew out.

The wolves snarled and looked around ... but in a moment, each of the three fell to the ground.

"Sleeping," said Umokuru. "Not dead. They'll remember."

"Young bucks," he said of the wolves. "They got two chickens last night. I knew they'd come back for more."

"How did you do that, great one?" asked Mahmoud.

Umokuru showed them the blow-dart.

"Master Umokuru," said Leo. "Can I see that weapon?"

They sat at a table near the staging area, in the shade of a grove of birch adjacent to the river bed.

"Why have you come to France?" asked Will while Leo inspected the weapon.

"Canals. Canals and bridges," answered the African. "Bridges and levees and dams."

Leo began take the blow-gun apart.

"A young girl of the Ashanti," the African continued, "designs and builds all manner of structures. She has her people building a walled city with towers and schools and kitchens and baths. Now she wants to build canals and bridges in my home, Benin.

"She will transform the western kingdoms. She needs maps. My niece and I are here to study the Canal and to make copies of all the maps Jalmari has in her stacks. Then we return. Before war starts."

"War over what?" asked Mahmoud.

"Over the girl. The architect. The Masai have set out to kill her. The African thrones have noticed what she brings their people.

"Her brother has raised an army to protect her."

"This architect. What is her name?"

"Yaa Asantewa," answered Umokuru.

"I have it!" exclaimed Leo.

* * *

After dinner that night, Leo and Mahmoud asked to see Umokuru. Frestel came as well.

Leo showed them a pistol he had modified as they walked out to the west barn, at the edge of the orchards, where Leo and Mahmoud had set up a sort of firing range, complete with roped off lanes and brightly colored targets.

Umokuro hefted the pistol.

"Is this the new gun?" asked Frestel.

"The new bullets, more like," replied Leo. "Try it."

Umokuru raised the gun three times before he fired.

"Good God." He muttered an oath, a blistering generational curse sometimes heard among the Bantu.

He shot again. The target tore.

Frestel shot. He corrected and shot again, then once more, shredding the target. He let go an exclamation.

"How does it do that?" Frestel asked the students.

"See here?" replied Mahmoud. "Look – the base of Master U's dart is made from pith. The spongy wood, from the center of the tree trunk.

"Leo tried the junipers and the cherries until he found a spruce –now it does the same for the bullet as it does for the blow-dart..

"The pith expands into the tube," explained Leo, "closing the gap between the tube and the dart – the gun barrel and the bullet – so the range is increased,

"Then I took apart the gun barrel and scored it slightly, see here, so that the bullet rotates as it shoots forward. It comes out spinning. Stays on course."

"So." The African held the gun before him. "Trapped gas for velocity, rotating bullet for stable trajectory."

"The trajectory doesn't loop quite as much ..." added Leo.

Once he corrected, Umokuru and did not miss the next six shots

"Eye-koh-na!" exclaimed Umokuru, followed by a series of click-sounds and tongue-knocks.

"It stays straighter longer!" said Frestel.

"The rotation steadies its course," added Mamhoud, who had helped.

"You must make me one," said Frestel.

At the first sounds of shooting, the monkeys had fled to higher ground. Now they returned, cautiously.

* * *

One night they all sat in the library beneath the many wall-lanterns and hanging lights.

"You don't miss much," said Gilbert of Mei Ying's sketches. They showed various details of the canal, and how each was assembled.

"It is part of my mission," replied Mei Ying. "My family wants to build ones like this in the hills of Zunhua, where the canal does not reach."

"I will also buy several circuits of those new seeds, too," continued Mei Ying. "I know a woman in Zhangzhou who trades in seeds -- "

"What's this?" Leo asked Mahmoud.

"The dictionary of the American Indians" replied the Ottoman prince. "The only one in existence, or so says Jalmari. They have charts for the Iroquois sign language -- "

"Leo!" said Will from one of the alcoves. "I've found a section with all the Alsace-Lorraine records. Even two of the southern German baronies. Alsace has changed hands many times. You need to see -- "

Leo yawned, making a show of his disregard. He preferred to invent impossible weapons, and draw them in great detail, sometimes making noises to accompany.

"*Si vis pacem, para bellum*," Will warned Leo gravely.

"Must it always be in Latin?" groaned Leo.

"Only the important things," replied Will.

CHAPTER 16

A Letter Arrives

We little know how much
of the uncontrollable there is in us.

-- John Muir

"IT'S SO HEAVY-- "

Shay was resisting taking full part in the target practice which Leo had organized to demonstrate his innovation.

"Come, Queen of the Volga," said Leo. "You never know when you'll need it -- "

Shay took a shot. The pistol bucked. The rotating bullet skimmed straight into the highest of the hay bales beyond the target, missing entirely.

"Grip it tight!" insisted Leo. "Quit complaining!"

"You jerked it—" advised Mahmoud, acting as Leo's second.

"Listen to Leo," said Gilbert. "This is a wonder. He has reconfigured it so that it shoots like one of Umokuru's darts -- "

"You heard what Master Dubin said," continued Leo. "This is a dangerous game we play -- "

Shay chuffed at this overly dramatic analysis. Reluctantly, she let Will show her how to squeeze the trigger without yanking it back ...

Mei Ying was not so reluctant. She blasted three of the targets to shreds once she got the hang of it.

* * *

A letter arrived.

It was for Gilbert. The markings on the well-weathered envelope said that it came from America.

74

Gilbert opened it.

A pair of African peacocks dodged the glancing rubber balls which caromed off the stone walls, trying to preserve some measure of dignity as they sauntered through the courtyard where the students sat waiting for dinner.

The noisy young Spanish cousins, Dukes of the Catalan provinces, wearing big padded gloves on their hands, chased loudly after the balls, which landed with a splash in the fountain. Leo and Mahmoud were playing cards.

"Read it, Gilbert," said Clotilde, but Gilbert refused. She took it.

"It's from Boston," she said. "From Gilbert's cousin, Joincare -- see the mud stains on the envelope, it must have come directly from the battlefield!" She read the letter aloud. Here is what it said, in part:

> *Yesterday I watched a fellow soldier amputate his own infected foot. Today we spent our morning rooting for mushrooms, and this afternoon I set out on an expedition with Captain Parminter, to the Hudson Valley. It is five days' journey, and we have few provisions.*

> *Yet I feel closer to my true heart here, among these desperate privations and these plain men, than I ever did in the cushioned parlors of Europe. God blesses our cause, Cousin. I know we will triumph --*

A sudden furious thrashing overhead silenced the courtyard.

All the young nobles looked upwards.

A hawk had launched itself at the peacocks, only to become ensnared in the netting which protected the courtyard aviary. They could see the hawk blazing eyes, almost close enough to touch: this was no heraldic symbol, no cooing pet, but a bird of prey whose razor-sharp claws gave clear proof of its deadly intent towards the peacocks. The hawk had swooped in on the strutting ground birds, only to become entangled in a web it did not see or understand. The wild bird thrashed furiously, hissing and spitting at its would-be prey.

Servants climbed over the netting. With some effort, the hawk would be collected and removed.

The handball game resumed. The dulcimer counterpoints of Bach again filled the courtyard.

Mahmoud lay down his cards. Leo protested, in vivid Teutonic phrases. Mahmoud chuckled and collected the coins on the table.

"*It is we who are the peacocks,*" announced Gilbert with a fine disgust, to no one in particular. "My cousin is right. I would rather die fighting honorably than to live as we do: pets in this silken cage."

He rose from his seat and walked off.

The comment hung in the air.

Bells rang. Dinner was served. Mei Ying and Will had cooks' duty, so it promised to be a good one.

In the netting above, the falconers freed the hawk.

The peacocks came out of hiding.

* * *

"I've got to go home," was all Leo said when Mahmoud and Will returned to their rooms and saw that he had packed all his belongings.

Sheyndil sat on the edge of the stuffed chair, holding the letter Leo had received that day from his sister.

"Their father has taken ill," she said. "His drinking. And the serfs have petitioned the Prefecture to remove Leo's family of all their titles and holdings. Here is their list of demands ..."

She read them – seven demands in all (plus two requests).

"Leo has ninety days to resolve them."

She folded the letter and put it back in the envelope.

"And the sister – Romy -- has agreed to marry Lucien-- "

"*She needs me* -- " said Leo, with urgency. We all knew how much he cared for his elder sister.

"*You're being useless*, Leo" said Shay. "Is that what you want?"

"You need solutions to these problems."

She held the envelope and shook it at him, challenging him.

"That's what will help your sister."

"I may have an idea," said Will.

CHAPTER 17

A Late Night Talk

It was not until the 18th century that the commercial
use and monetization of data began in earnest,
most often attributed to the Dutch trading syndicates.

-- Saul Dubinsky, A Brief History of Botany

IT WAS IN THE VERY depths of the night, that brief, supernatural interval which transports all living things to the nether-world of slumbers, that a figure carried a lantern down the crooked hallways of the manor at *Nid de Corbeau.*

Shuffling over slanted wooden floorboards came Will O. He carried the lanterns in one hand and various ledgers and folders in the other.

He rapped on the door, softly but clearly.

Mme. Ovando opened the door.

"I beg your pardon, Mistress," said Will. "Most sincerely. May I speak to him?"

"Come in, come in, son ... "

"Master Dubin," said Will, his voice and demeanor were uncharacteristically clear and assertive.

"This is unforgivable, I know ..."

They sat at the kitchen table. Mme. Ovando lit the stove to prepare tea.

"I have discovered a cache of receipts. In the archives. Receipts, payments, actual florin notes, promissory notes, letters of credit, deposit slips.

"There exists a treasure in cash alone of more than ..."

Will slid across the table a piece of paper with a scribbled number. "This much. And if you add the value of the equities, it is thrice that, at least, and that does not count the VOC shares –" He shook his head in disbelief, as though he hoped to be told it was a mistake.

"It is a fortune -- "

"Many fortunes" corrected Dubin.

"And I have not even cleared the fourth batch -- "

Dubin, unsurprised at this news, rubbed his feet.

"But why do you ignore it, Master?"

Mme. Ovando shuffled around the pantry. The lone lantern's cone of light was joined by light from three other lanterns.

Dubin began to answer, but could not formulate his thoughts.

His wife served tea.

They drank in silence, the three of them, seated at a wooden circle, beneath a gabled roof, in a forest, near a Roman canal, beneath the blue-and-silver kingdoms of night.

"We have not ignored them, Will," said Dubin at length.

"The financials are well kept. Safe. Organized. We have categorized and indexed them, as they were sent to us."

"Yes, I can see that," argued Will. "But who gave all this to you?"

"The Oirates," answered Dubin. "The Swedes. Grateful pilots. A Spanish trading group which does business in the Far Indies-- "

"Why? What for?"

"They ask for charts, Will. Journals. Maps of currents. Anchorages."

"You give it to them?"

"No. We give them copies."

"For money?"

"For free."

"In return, some give us their thanks," continued Dubin. "In rubies. In consignments. Percentages. Monies that they imagine they owe to us. Using our charts, they save entire cargoes, you see. Using our data, they forecast prevailing winds and hiding storms, the depths of bays, late seasons, monsoons, when to sail and when to dock. That sort of thing. When to plant and when to lay fallow. You'd be surprised -- "

"Not any more," said Will. "Do you mean to say you have been given percentages of entire ships' cargos?"

"Six or seven, yes. The idea is -- "

"*Six* or *seven*?" exclaimed Will.

"The idea is that that our maps saved the entire voyage from sinking, you see." Dubin held out his hands, in a pantomime of helplessness.

"We never ask for compensation."

Mme. Ovado set out biscuits. Will took a bite; there were raisins hidden inside.

The ticking of the clock seemed to echo loudly. Dubin leaned down to feed the fire with logs. Flames rose and crackled.

"Why have you left the funds untouched? With such assets -- "

"Do dolphins have money?" asked Dubin.

"Do camels or mountain lions sign contracts? Do they carry money belts and bank tallies?

"Do whales? Do birds?

"Do florins grow into wheat, or flowers or berries, when you plant them in the soil?"

"Yes, I know all of that," said Will, exasperated. "But this could do much good. Think of it, Master ..."

"I am not Master," said Dubin, with a new tone in his voice, as if they had at last come to the heart of the matter.

"I am not Master. I sit in the chair. For now. I am caretaker until another comes along."

"And now you have come along," said Mme. Ovando sweetly.

That is the moment, that is the place, that is the statement, when the locks tumbled into place within young Will O. He would not forget it. He would never forget it.

"Do you mean to say you have been given percentages of entire ships' cargos?" Will asked. "Six or seven, yes," replied Dubin.

"You do it, Will," said Master Dubin.

"Take these, all this, to Amsterdam. You and Johannes. You can write a document giving you control over the funds.

"Use it for the good, son.

"All the Navigators wish it."

That night and the next, Will sat out on the broad ledge of the third-floor rooms, considering the silver stars and red orbiting planets and fiery hurling comets and contented satellite moons far, far above.

Seeing her friend so distracted, Shay sat with him.

Never a word was spoken.

Seeing Shay, the others joined.

CHAPTER 18

Mei Ying Calls

Ad utrumque paratus. Prepared for either.

-- Publius Vergilius Maro

"I HAVE MET YOUR KIND," said Mme. Ovando with a smile.

"Orientals, I mean."

"No doubt," replied Jiayi Mei Ying.

Mme. Ovando handed her grand-daughter to the little blonde house-maid.

The doors to the parlor closed behind them.

"Thank you for seeing us," said Mei Ying.

"Of course. Your French is excellent."

"We won't stay long.

"Madame. The Dubins and their circle -- my friends -- are scholars. Engineers. Collectors. Naturalists.

"They know little of the world.

"They are trusting.

"I am not.

"If anyone should attempt to take advantage of them, or try to take what they own, as you are seeking to, the repercussions will be dramatic.

"Specifically," said Mei Ying. She removed a long-bladed hunting knife from a sheath hidden along one leg, beneath her skirts. She laid the knife on the sofa cushion, between herself and Mme. Ovando. Its serrated blade looked incongruous resting against the quilted rose-petal fabric.

"I will personally cut your throat.

"And if I cannot, he will."

Teng Sho gave a nod.

Mei Ying stood.

"Now. We will let you get back to your granddaughter."

CHAPTER 19

The Siege

Every now and then a trigger
has to be pulled.

-- Robert Wade

AT MIDNIGHT THE NEXT NIGHT, as they lay in wait, Frestel glanced at Mei Ying.

"We had to challenge them. Our company will soon be disbanded, with the completion of the Canal, and Dubin will be left alone.

"We had no choice but to poke the bear. Your little talk forces their hand -- "

"Then where are they?" worried Mei Ying. "Why have they not-- "

It was the last night of the full moon. The Ovando raid on *Nid de Corbeau*, if it was ever going to happen would happen now.

A sound.

Shifting masses and careless noises on the other side of the stone wall signaled that the enemy was about to come over the rise.

"Steady, children," said Frestel in a low voice,

"Don't call me that," said Mahmoud. The moonlight caught the leaves all around him, turning them almost white.

"Call me El-Haroun."

"All right."

"What does 'Ill-Haroon' mean?" hissed Leo.

"The Avenger."

"Very well, Avenger," said Frestel. "Now we draw first blood --

"*Ad utrumque paratus!*" snarled Gilbert as his sword cleared its sheath. The phrase sounded familiar, almost calming, belying its meaning.

They entered the yard.

Wordlessly, the two sides clashed.

Using weapons modified with Leo's grooved bones and rotating bullet, three Dubin riflemen cut down three of the first-wave raiders.

A pistol clattered on the stone steps, then another. A body fell heavily, with the sound of moaning.

The invaders kept trying to swarm and capture first Sheyndil, then Gilbert --

"The girl!" shouted Chugunov.

Gilbert struck at him with his open sword -- Chugunov parried, and his two companions rushed to aid him --

Shay opened fire with pistol, aimed directly at Chugunov's chest. Her volley knocked him over the stone retaining wall.

An attacker grabbed Shay from behind.

"*Let go of her!*" Will demanded --

As he spoke, a gun roared and a bullet whistled past his head.

Will saw several figures descend on her, cutting her off from the rest of us. Bullets were still flying --

Will rolled over in the garden bed and came up with the knife Mei Ying had given him in his hand.

He flung it low, at the group of invaders, to the left of where he could see his friend --

The blade found its mark; Will heard a pained grunt.

A pistol shot from one of the hidden library windows sounded and another of the raiders fell.

Leo's rotating bullets found their mark.

Shay freed herself --

Two remaining kidnappers retreated to the footbridge, unaware that it led only to the raised gardens, and they were trapped. A swordsman appeared: Frestel parried with the pair while Gilbert called out in several languages for the kidnappers to give up and flee, or risk their lives.

"The barn!" called Mahmoud.

Pierre Ovando raced towards the barns, torch in hand.

Mahmoud fired and missed.

A second group rushed from the defenders' southern flank towards Leo and Mahmoud.

The Ottoman Prince fired his pistol --

Leo caught a blade with a hand he had wrapped in leather, and yanked the sword away – the marauder fell backwards into the stream.

A second followed him into the water as Mei Ying flung him off her back and over the railing --

Goats and chickens and sleepy cattle scattered at the melee.

A new band of monarchists came from the woods. A frenzy of clicks and clanging blades and whistles rose as Umokuru and his niece, stationed in the underbrush, made quick work.

Another quartet had been trapped on the garden bridge

They saw the white of Master Frestel's smile flashing in the moonlight.

"Fire!"

The wind shifted. They could see the orange light rising in the night. They could hear in the distance a panic among the horses, accompanied by pigs squealing and monkeys chattering.

"Fire in the barn -- "

It was Master Dubin's voice.

With renewed energy, they fell on the attackers.

The monarchists, disorganized now that their initial rush had failed, did not seem to have a plan. So many guns used against them with deadly force seemed to surprise them.

Frestel felled Michel Ovando, their leader.

Bodies tumbled.

One of the monarchists turned and fled. He beckoned the others.

Golden flames lit up a section of the night.

"Will!" cried Shay, beset by monarchists –

"Get Tessa-- "

Flames poured out of the barn's loft and spread quickly to the paddocks. The monkeys watched from the tree crowns.

Pierre Ovando held a torch aloft.

They could see his features, twisted in hatred.

A last clutch of monarchists descended on Shay. Frestel drew a gun on one of them and he fell with a groan.

Leo struck the sword from another invader's hand and ended with his arm tight around the man's neck; he twisted hard and the man dropped, inert.

Water from the troughs came in a line. The livestock were led to the back pastures, where reflected light outlined the giraffes, watching, munching.

Dubin poured bucket after bucket into the flames. The wood caught so fast --

A last attacker leapt at Frestel.

Mei Ying flung her dagger. The man fell hard --

The fire abated.

The monarchists fled.

Jalmari appeared, dragging one of the Hungarians who had tried to lay siege to the library tower.

Umukoru came up from the vegetable patches, Ovando the Younger himself in tow.

"Report!"called Frestel.

"Marchand has been wounded," declared Mahmoud, naming one of the farmhands.

Gilbert kneeled beside the figure with the straight-bladed dagger in his neck. He was a Hungarian; his face was familiar, they had seen him at the market that day.

"Is he dying?" asked Shay.

"Aye," answered Gilbert.

The Hungarian flayed on his back like a fish, choking for breath that would not come. Dubin removed the blade, but too much damage had been done.

They could see now that he was no more than a boy.

Jara murmured the last rites over him.

Dubin spoke to him in another language.

The boy nodded.

"*Tell my sister --* " whispered the Hungarian. "She lives in the village of Szent Skanzen-- "

"Aye. I know of the place," said Dubin. "We will tell her you died bravely."

The boy seemed to relax. He blinked at Shay. "I have some coins – she will be waiting – *Ugh! No!* "

Mahmoud swore bitterly.

"Don't die. Please!" Will cried. "This is *horrible --*"

Leo had gone ashen-faced.

The Hungarian boy gave a final shiver and passed to a better world.

Frestel shut the boy's eyelids.

Slowly, he stood. He turned to Ovando.

"Blood has been spilled tonight," said Frestel, in a voice so fraught with deadly emotion they did not recognize it at first.

"*Na yige*," demanded Teng Sho. He looked from Michel Ovando to the son, Pierre.

"*No!*" screamed Shay.

Gilbert escorted her back to the paddocks, so she could tend the animals.

Teng Sho clutched the father tightly by the throat; Frestel held the son.

"Which is it to be?" asked Frestel.

"Me," croaked Michel Ovando, whose face had lost all color, whose voice had lost all tone.

"Let my son live."

The son begged for mercy until Teng Sho blasted him across the jaw, for it was the son who had lit the barn on fire.

Then, deliberate in his movements, Master Frestel waved off everyone, even Umukoru. Even Gilbert

He and Teng Sho took Lord Ovando and disappeared into the woods.

The others escorted the Ovando son westward, towards his home.

The silhouettes merged with the shadows.

Mei Ying had not been seen since flinging the dagger that saved Gilbert ...

CHAPTER 20:

The Pact

Nothing except a battle lost
can be half so melancholy as a battle won.

-- The First Duke of Wellington

LATER THAT SAME NIGHT, MEI Ying appeared as the friends dug the Hungarian's grave out behind the barn, on a slight bluff near the first rows of the orchard.

The safe, blanketing sound of crickets had settled on the night. Burbling water sounds of the mill stream accompanied the celestial display above.

They shoveled in silence, each considering the events of the night. The Malay monkeys who lived in the barn came to watch the burial, along with a camel and a sleepy-eyed giraffe.

A tall figure appeared, carrying a lantern in one hand and a satchel over his shoulder. The monkeys scattered.

It was Master Frestel.

He looked around at their work.

"I must say Good-bye."

His students blinked in the star-lit midnight, not understanding.

"I am leaving the school. Tonight. For Boston.

"I will raise my banner, such as it is, with the Americans, and add my colors to theirs. They fight for us all.

"I wish each of you good luck. We may not meet again."

Will burst into tears.

"Come, Dutchman. This is what I am meant for. I am no teacher."

Master Frestel spoke a few words privately to each of them.

Sheyndil removed the blue scarf from her neck and gave it to him.

Then, with a wave, Master Frestel left the Royal Academy at *Nid de Corbeau*, walking fearlessly into the maw of night, much as Achilles had walked that night long ago on the beaches of Troy, striding from the campfires into the shadows of the forces of Menelaus and Agamemnon ... or so it seemed to the youth whom he left behind.

"I have never felt more alone," said Mahmoud.

They watched him descend the path down along the creek, where moonlight reflected, and then into the meadows, moving among the shadows of the beasts, until they could no longer make out his form, until all they could see was a bobbing light, and even when that vanished, they kept watching.

Tessa's foal stumbled out of the barn door to find where everyone had gone.

Sheyndil wrapped the foal in a blanket and carried it back to the barn.

They finished filling the grave. The sound of the shovel blades on the dirt as they patted it down seemed comforting.

"What did he say to you, Sheyndil?" I asked when she returned.

The others stopped digging to listen to her reply.

"He said I was a gift to the Russian people, and that it was up to me to protect myself."

"I'm scared," said Will.

"He told me that war is more than glinting swords and waving banners," said Leo. "He told me that I was like him. Hard-headed. And that such men as we must take care that our volatile natures do not lead us astray."

Mahmoud took a deep breath, and shuddered.

"He told me not to worry, that I would find my place in the world, among honest men" said Gilbert, as he stared at some unseen point in the starry distance.

Crickets and other night sounds filled the yard. The giraffe watched, curious, crunching on high-branch leaves without conviction, for he did not really care to eat at night.

Spades patted the earth.

When they had finished the grave, Sheyndil took each by the sleeve.

She gathered the friends, under the stars.

"*We must make a pact,*" she said, her eyes glistening in the moonlight.

Shay put out her hand. They all did the same, even Teng Sho, and the seven clasped trembling hands together there, over the new grave, over life and death, there beneath glittering Gemini and Sagittarius, there among the barn monkeys and the horses and the towering giraffe.

They took an oath.

"Let us always remember tonight. How we fought for one another, and risked our lives.

"Let us always be honest with one another.

"Let us band together in this regard: we will always try to do good, and never be selfish."

Tears ran down Shay's face as she spoke, but her voice was clear and certain.

"And any one of us who gets into trouble – *real trouble* – can send for the others. The others must come, at any expense.

"If one of us calls, the others must answer. We each vow it," she said, with deepest conviction, and then she repeated this to each in turn, and made each repeat it for themselves, and held Gilbert's face so as to force him to look into her eyes as he swore it.

At the little ceremony's end, under the stars, Leo mistakenly said *Sic Semper Tyrannus* as a sort of codicil, but not even Mahmoud objected, for its defiant tone seemed to suit the moment.

Afterword

In an address to the Organization of American Historians some time ago, OAH President James Oliver Horton argued that if the promise of America is to be fulfilled, its people must understand its history. He called for a new generation of historians to place America in its rightful context, a *global* context – to portray U.S. history not as a story separated from the rest of the world, but as part of a world narrative.

This story – the story of the American Revolution – is like that. Beneath the popular tales of the American Revolution lies a larger and more complex narrative – a global narrative. I am not smart enough to tell it, but I am happy to suggest it in this little adventure.

At the same time the Swamp Fox was raiding Cornwallis in the Carolina lowlands, French and British forces fought five naval battles off the coast of India. Concurrent to the Colonials crossing the Delaware to surprise Von Donop, the two largest German states, Austria and Prussia, established an "enlightened absolutism" and fought to push one another out of the German Federation. Between Pontiac's Rebellion and Washington's inauguration, the population of China ballooned to 300 million with the introduction of potatoes and peanuts from America, while the Emperor's eldest son perpetuated some of the worst corruption in the history of the Qing Dynasty.

The American Revolution was fought in the world. All of this played a part.

One view or theory connecting these global forces is the coming of the modern age: that the industrial revolution was bringing an economic end to the slave trade, and the beginning of full rights for all. In books like *Empire* and *Colossus*, one of my favorite historians, Niall Ferguson, paints the picture of a world of rising empires and falling cultures, a world convulsed by global economic forces, and social forces set into motion by the engines of modern production.

The statement in my story by Catherine the Great's disciple, Sheyndil, regarding botany and the American Revolution, represents a school of thought suggested by Andrea Wulf in her outstanding 2011 book, *Founding Gardeners: The Revolutionary Generation, Nature, and the Shaping of the American Nation*. One of the many ideas she brings into her book is that "it's impossible to understand the making of America without looking at the founding fathers as farmers and gardeners."

This botany-and-empire connection is given a fuller expression by a character named Saul Dubinsky, who appears in a subsequent adventure. Dubinsky becomes caretaker of the Navigator archives and their unique contents, and it is he who narrativizes several of the Society adventures.

* * *

In movies, there can be such a thing as "the male gaze." This is when the camera sees things as males see them. A neutral camera would not act that way. There may be such a thing as a national gaze, narratives in which a nation looks at a universe that is centered around that particular unit of civilization.

Historian Larrie D Ferreiro thinks a little bit of this may have crept into our telling of our own history, particularly the story of the American Revolution. We tend to make ourselves the hero of what is a complex, sprawling story. It suits us to downplay or neglect to mention critical help we received from Europe. A neutral, or more universal version might be different.

"The involvement of other nations in the conflict was largely erased from the historical record," Ferreiro writes. This is not so much a studied effort as it is a natural tendency to want to establish our own cultural identity – American exceptionalism.

We tend to make ourselves the heroes of what is a complex, sprawling story.

Others make the same point. "If there is one big meta-trend within history, it is this turn toward the global," says Sven Beckert, Laird Bell Professor of American History at Harvard University. "History looks very different if you don't take a particular nation-state as the starting point of all your investigations."

As new ideas of the Enlightenment swept across the world, the American rebels joined people of many nations who were looking for a new relationship to empire. We now connect the Boston Tea Party to the Sepoy Rebellion in India as well as to the Irish Rebellion, the Latin American wars of independence, and the Decembrist revolt in Russia.

* * *

In "The Illustrated Colonials," I have willfully ignored accurate dates and names and sequences. I have invented characters and events in order to serve my low-brow adventure.

My inclusion of an earlier version of the Minie bullet is ridiculous. As all my cadets will tell you, this is the bullet that changed the Civil War, not the Revolutionary War.

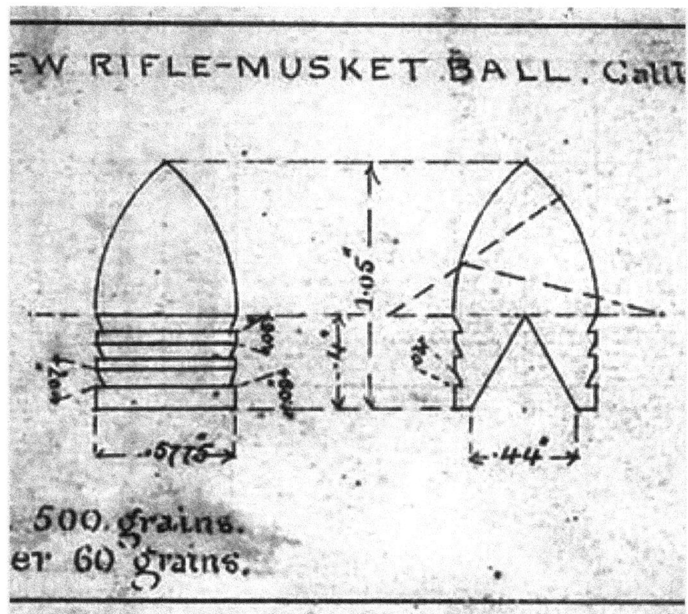

You should also know that the Emancipation Edicts of the Yongzheng reign (1723-1735) were not quite as compatible with Thomas Paine as I make it out. These were aimed at the *jiang*, the outcast peoples, and not the sweeping equality that Paine envisioned. Yet I am on solid ground, I think, to link the Colonial version of equality to other movements around the globe.

One aspect less-told is the Native American war within the Revolution. It was the Native American tribes' war as well as anyone's. What would it look like if the story were told from that viewpoint, I wonder.

I completely ignore the Spanish contribution. Also, my version of the Battle of Cuddalore, often termed "the last battle of the American Revolution," did not make it into these three volumes. Maybe in a fourth volume.

Once Leo walked out of the plotline I had devised for him and sailed for Africa, I did not find a character to tell the Hessian side of things.

* * *

As clever readers have guessed, I provide a wealth of excellent illustrations in this volume in order to distract you from my failings as a writer. I have asked each of the illustrators to present their own interpretations of my story's characters and events. They make me look good. The day is mine.

I want to thank several of my teachers for their generosity: Robert Ashcom and Jerry Whitson (Pem-Day); Chuck Sanborn, Coaches Alexander and Conley, and Rudy Weber (Mount Hermon); G.D. Stagg, D.M. Summerscale, A.S. White, Oliver van Oss and J.C. Phillips (Charterhouse).

I hope you will visit my websites for more --

Tom Durwood
Valley Forge, PA

www.mycolonials.com
www.empirestudiespress.com
www.boatmansdaughter.com

The cause of America is in a great measure the cause of all mankind. Many circumstances have, and will arise, which are not local, but universal ...

Thomas Paine

THE ILLUSTRATED COLONIALS

Home Fronts
Book Two

Durwood takes one of history's
greatest events and retells it through
these six wonderful, authentic, and
deeply relatable characters.
-- *Sara Ridley, Life of a Storyteller book blog*

The meticulously rendered
illustrations ... shimmer
with depth and feeling.
-- *Prairies Book Review*

PROLOGUE

RULE ONE: MASS. CONCENTRATE COMBAT power at the decisive time and place.

Gilbert du Motier, late of the Selestat Academy, stood in a kitchen in a stone farmhouse in the Pennsylvania territory of the American continent. It was two hours until dawn. His rifle lay against the kitchen counter.

Rule Two: Objective. Direct every military operation towards a clearly defined, decisive and attainable objective.

He would soon be marching into his first battle. Very soon now.

Gilbert had spent most of the previous night bent over in the bushes, wretching from fear of facing bullets meant to kill him. His stomach felt twisted and empty. His head was dizzy. He had not slept. He felt weak, and sick; his legs could scarcely hold his body's weight. Empty phrases ran through his mind, the rules of war which he had learned at school.

Rule Three: Offensive. Seize, retain and exploit the initiative.

The three colonial soldiers who had been assigned to protect the Frenchman ate in silence, standing at counter in the Quaker's kitchen. The farmer, Gilpin half-heartedly complained that Congress would never repay him for the fifty pounds of bacon he was contributing to the colonial cause. *Fifteen thousand heavily armed British troops lay across the creek on this man's property, and we are about to die taking up arms to defend him,* thought Gilbert, *and all he can think of his fifty pounds of bacon...*

This was not what he thought it would be. His was not how Gilbert imagined battle. *Rule Five: Surprise. Strike the enemy at a time, at a place, or in a manner for which he is unprepared.*

Gilbert could not remember the fourth rule of war. Was it 'economy of force'? *Damn everything,* thought Gilbert, *if only Mahmet were here --*

* * *

On this pretty Pennsylvania morning, the British commander, General William Howe and the Hessian Lieutenant General, Wilhelm von Knyphausen, were coming with three heavily-armed brigades to kill Gilbert and all his colonial friends.

As Gilbert and companions stood waiting, sodden and shivering and exhausted, in the pre-dawn darkness, a long line of red-coated Queen's Rangers, Ferguson's riflemen, and members of the 16th Light Dragoons moved steadily towards the stream-bed below Gilpin's farmhouse. They came from the west. At their vanguard was an advance party, to clear any obstacles the colonials might have set in their path. Behind them were the First and Second British Brigades, followed by the artillery and supply wagons, and livestock which they had commandeered, or stolen, from local farmers. A New Jersey colonial who saw the force from the safety of Welch's Tavern called it "a sight beyond description grand."

Gilbert inched down the meadow which sloped from the Quaker farmhouse to the creek, gripping his rifle tight in the pre-dawn darkness. The creek had been dammed, and its stench rose to surround him. His stomach turned.

"Careful," whispered his sergeant, as Gilbert stepped on a twig and snapped it. "The redcoats are listening ... "

And they are eager to make you their first victim, he might have added, for the English knew of Gilbert's presence among the colonials.

It was 4 o'clock in the morning.

Gilbert had imagined combat as the paintings depict it: an heroic undertaking on a sunny day, with pipers playing on the grassy knoll, and banners waving, the enemy neatly arrayed down the slope and his comrades standing close by his side. This was ... unseemly. This was ... squalid, and forlorn. The 'battlefield' was little more than a common creek: they would be chasing the enemy through thickets, like squirrels, and firing from behind hiding-places behind fence-posts. *A single lucky ball from a Fusilier's muzzle can mangle my face*, Gilbert thought, for the thousandth time, *or cripple me for life, or end my life now, before it has really begun.*

"Remember, if ye are wounded, keep yer eyes open," advised his companion. "The surgeons will not tend any man whose eyes are closed ..."

Merciful God, what have I done? Gilbert du Motier asked himself.

Merciful God, what have I done? Gilbert du Motier asked himself.

* * *

The battle began as a series of skirmishes. The British would dart forward, fire from cover of a tree, and fall back. The Colonials fired from behind every advantageous post or fence or outcropping.

After the sun rose, the entire British line advanced, slowly, at a great expense in lives, amid a galling fire and dense smoke which choked off the morning sunlight.

"What excessive fatigue," one participant would later recall. "'Twas not like those at Covent Garden or Drury Lane – there was most infernal fire of cannon and musket, and most incessant shouting, 'Incline to the right!' 'Incline to the left!' 'Halt!' 'Charge!' The musket balls ploughed up the ground. Trees cracked over one's head, the branches riven by artillery, the leaves fell as in autumn, by the grapeshot ..."

As the bullets plunked into the ground, Gilbert du Motier stood terrified.

If only Mahmoud were here ... He would know.

The Colonials seemed to look up to Gilbert, as a Frenchman, as a European. They seemed to expect him to have some special knowledge of battles involving British forces. Yet he had none. He was a fraud. He stroked the barrel of his rifle, as if to clean it. He straightened the jacket of his uniform.

I don't want to die, thought Gilbert.

He spotted a redcoat through the green foliage.

He raised his rifle and fired.

The recoil hurt his shoulder; the powder left a nasty, metal taste in his mouth.

He had missed.

He rushed forward to kill the man, cursing King George and all his followers.

His two handlers, who had been told to keep the young French nobleman out of the battle as long as possible, ran after Gilbert as he hurtled headlong down the slope towards the creek, and towards his enemy, as Pericles had done so long ago, on the beaches of Sybota.

His own efforts, like the Colonial war effort at large, seemed doomed.

Who could save them?

* * *

Around 10:30 the firing slowed.

Knyphausen, who had been told by Howe to make it appear that the entire British force were with him, ordered his men to march back and forth among the hills and cow paths on the creek's western side.

The American general, George Washington, did not know what was happening.

The colonial force was smaller than the British company, with far less artillery, and they husbanded their resources too carefully.

The reports were so contradictory, so confusing, that Washington did not know where the enemy's true strength lay. At noon, he made a decision: mistakenly believing that the British strength lay to the north, he ordered a substantial portion of his light infantry to cross the river at Chadd's Ford and engage the British 49th regiment. Downstream, at Pyle's Ford, a regiment of Pennsylvania militiamen joined the fray. A huge column of British troops – 8,000 men – previously hidden to the colonials now emerged to the rear of the Americans' right flank and was about to attack from the north. The Americans sent three brigades dashing north, to form a line along Birmingham Road.

The two sides were now face-to-face across the creek.

The Americans rallied, and managed to form a second defensive line 800 yards southwest of the initial encounter.

The Pennsylvania militia held the left flank.

Howe rode to from Osborne Hill to Birmingham Hill, to better direct the battle.

Amid fierce fighting, the American line gave way again and again times, re-forming only to fall further back. The officers "exerted themselves beyond description to keep up," wrote their commander, General John Sullivan of New Hampshire. "Five times did the enemy drive our troops from the hill, and as often was it regained, the summit often disputed muzzle to muzzle."

And muzzle to muzzle it continued, long into that death-filled day. Sullivan sent frantic messages to Washington, begging for reinforcements. Washington held off, in the mistaken belief that the main British force was still north of them, with Knyphausen.

Till dark the two armies fought, up and down the river, amid severe cannonading. At the end, seven thousand lay dead. The Continental Army still existed; the rebellion still lived.

The Colonial war effort seemed doomed. *Who could save them?*

Gilbert fought with great courage, imploring light corps commanded by the veteran colonial commander Sullivan to allow him to lead the light corps across the creek and directly into the British strength. He did not slow when an enemy shot wounded him in the leg. The colonials were glad to have this dashing young Frenchman fighting at their side at that battle near the Quaker farm, a battle later to be known by the name of the creek, which the locals called Brandywine

Home Fronts, Book Two of *The Illustrated Colonials*, is scheduled for publication on June 22, 2021.

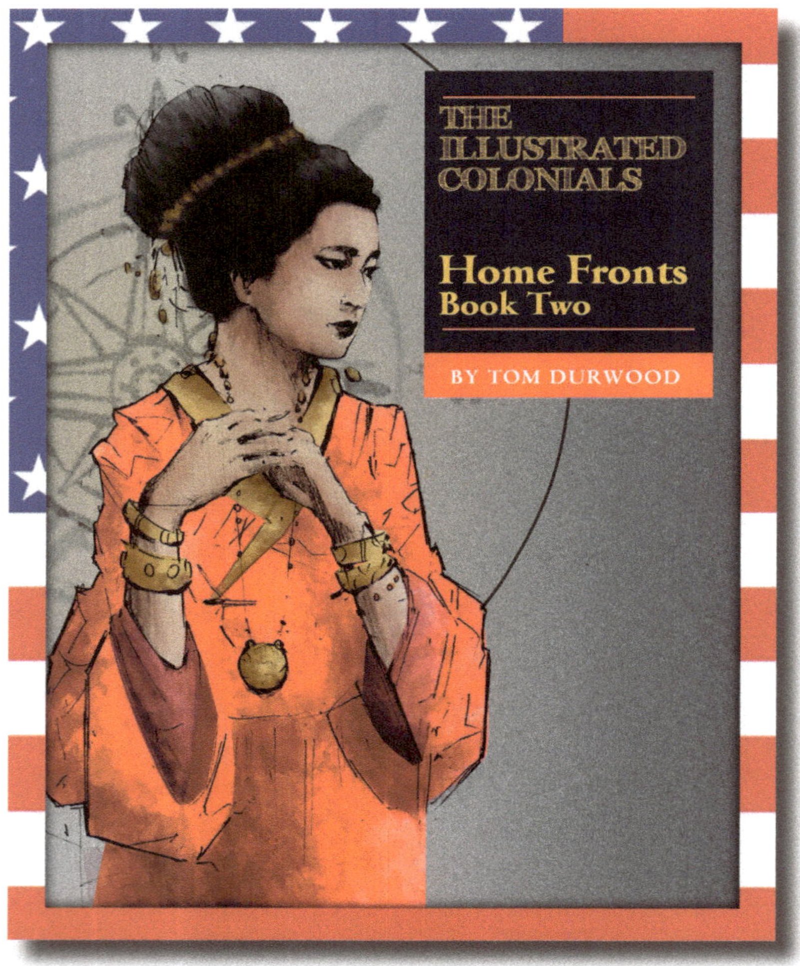

Purchase your copy today wherever books are sold to continue your adventure with the Colonials.
Visit www.mycolonials.com for more.